日常 如何活用
英文單字
How to Effectively Use Everyday English Words

How to ?
Effectively Use Everyday
English Words

自序 Preface

　　「世界日報」是北美最有影響力、名氣最大、銷售最廣的中文日報，我能在該報的「世界週刊」寫了十四年的「實用英語」專欄，感到榮幸。

　　在這段時間裡，前六、七年所發表的文稿，承蒙台灣大名鼎鼎的聯經出版公司為我出了三本書（不包括一本在中國大陸發行的簡體版），我很開心。

　　我長期在美國生活，深深體會單字是英語學習中重要的一環，因此我將一些日常所見的單字，整理出他們相關的用法，讓讀者能夠活用自如。並包括了流行字詞、接合字，容易混淆的字詞以及記單字的一些方法，相信都能幫助擴充英語學習者的單字量。

　　出書是許多教育者的心願，由於每個人的需求和看法不同，本書要想「人人稱好」可不容易。但我盡量做到內容充實，深入淺出，使人一目瞭然。

　　我仍然維持「自我風格」，不請高官名人題字作序，不過我要感謝以下諸位：

- 聯經出版公司發行人林載爵先生對我文稿的興趣與採納。
- 北美世界書局總經理周才博先生對拙文的賞識和推薦。
- 專攻英美文學與寫作，深受大學裡同仁敬佩的 James Thrash 教授，在我疑難時，作出指點。
- 《世界週刊》主編常誠容女士的審核，使拙文生色不少。
- 聯經出版公司主編李芃女士的編審與協助，使本書趨於完善。

　　最後我感謝家人的鼓勵與支持。本書如能有助華人學習英語，是我最大的欣慰。

　　我仍用筆名「懷中」，因為我沒有忘記自己是中華兒女，在做人處事上，我仍以「中庸之道」自勉。

懷中

2012 年 7 月

目次 Contents

淺易單字活用

　　英文的單字可謂「千變萬化」，有的一個字，就有許多不同的意義；有的字，又可擔任句子裡不同的角色。美（英）國人喜歡把日常簡單的名詞當作動詞用，也把淺易的名詞或動詞，當作特別意義用。他們認為這樣才有「新鮮感」，也可以減少用字，簡化句子。

　　以下介紹的都是平時常見的單字，若能善加活用，學習生活上的英語，好處不盡。

Part 1　淺易單字活用

age

 001

名詞　指年齡、生命中一階段，或感到很長時間

例句

· This Chinese girl married an American of her father's age.
這位中國女孩嫁給一位她父親年齡的美國人。

· Mr. Wang likes to use age to prove his superiority.
王先生喜歡倚老賣老。

· Where have you been, John? I haven't seen you for ages.
John，你到那兒去了？我很久沒看到你。

動詞　變老、老化、變舊

例句

· After a major surgery, Mr. B has aged considerably.
經過一次大手術後，B 先生老多了。

· We are all aging as the days pass.（aging = ageing）
隨著日子的過去，我們都在老化。

· Constant worry may age a person.
常常憂愁，會使人老化。

· All appliances will continue to age every year.
所有的家庭用具，每年都會繼續變舊。

air

◀》 002

 名詞　空氣，或氣氛

例句

· Chinese people always like to open the windows and let some air into the rooms.
中國人喜歡開窗戶，使房間的空氣流通。

· Several years ago, the air between Taiwan and China grew rather tense.
數年前，台灣和中國間的氣氛，頗為緊張。

 動詞　通風；播出；晾衣服；表示意見

例句

· Please open some windows and air the overheated room.
請打開窗戶，讓這過熱的房間，通風一下。

· The 2012 Olympic opening celebration will be aired on NBC this Friday.
2012 年奧運會開幕典禮，將在本週五由 NBC 播出。

· You may fully air your opinion at the meeting.
開會時，你可充分表達高見。

· Many Chinese believe that it is healthful to air clothes out in the sun.
許多老中認為在太陽下曬衣服有益健康。

ax（或 axe）

🔊 003

 斧頭

例句

· I have no ax to grind over this issue.
  我對這個問題，沒有私心與怨言。

動詞 是削減（to cut），多半指經費或人員的減少（動詞時態是：axed, axing）

例句

· Mr. Bush is trying to ax billions of dollars from income taxes.
  布希先生設法削減億萬的所得稅。

· Axing taxes is always welcomed by the middle-class Americans.
  減稅都會受到中產階級的美國人所歡迎。
  （主詞 axing，也可用不定詞 to ax；如果用形容詞 welcome，那麼
   介系詞要用 to。）

· The school demands that any teacher with poor behavior be axed.
  學校要求任何行為不良的老師，都要解聘。
  （be axed = be fired）

· The college president has axed some administrative positions because of budget-cuts.
  由於預算削減，這所大學校長解雇一些行政人員。
  （has axed = has eliminated）

baby

 004

 嬰孩或年紀最小的人。

例句

- I would like to know who is the baby of your family.
  我想知道誰是府上年齡最小的。

 嬌縱，當作嬰兒般對待或細心照顧

例句

- She is trying to baby her sick husband.
  她細心照顧生病的丈夫。

- Over the past years, he babied his wife too much.
  過去多年來他過分嬌縱他的太座。

- She seemed to have babied herself when she was pregnant.
  看來她懷孕時對自己細心照料。

- We laughed about Mrs. Wang for babying her adult son.
  我們笑王太太把成年的兒子，當做嬰孩般地照顧。

bass

🔊 005

名詞 指「鱸魚」；「（音樂）低音」（發音：鱸魚 [bæs] 低音 [bes]）

例句

- The fisherman caught a lot of bass yesterday.
  漁夫昨天抓到很多鱸魚。

5

- He is a bass player in the band.
  他是樂隊裡的低音歌手。

- A bass was painted on the head of the bass drum.
  大鼓的上端畫有一隻鱸魚。
  （bass drum 是大鼓）

blue

🔊 006

 名詞 藍色；煩惱

例句

- The two blues are nearly the same.
  這兩種藍色幾乎一樣。

- Your warm hospitality has cured my blues.
  你的熱情招待消除了我的悶悶不樂。

- Many Americans have the "Monday Blues."
  許多美國人有「藍色星期一」的現象。
  （因為他們覺得週末太短，到了星期一就悶悶不樂，故有 "Monday Blues" 之稱，不過 blue 後面要加 s）

 形容詞 藍色的；憂鬱的

例句

- Her dress is blue.
  她的衣服是藍色。

· She felt blue this morning.
今早她意氣消沉。

· What is the point of feeling blue?
有什麼好難過的呢？

· He bought many blue chips.
他買了許多值錢而熱門的藍籌股票。

 使用藍色漂白劑

例句

· Laundries blue clothes in different ways.
洗衣店以不同方法使用可防止白色衣物泛黃的藍色漂白劑。

· Bluing the clothes is a method in the laundry business.
在洗衣的行業裡，使用藍色漂白劑是方法之一。

 once in a blue moon 表示「極少」「罕見」

例句

· His visit to the U.S. is once in a blue moon.
他來美訪問是很難得的。

book

 007

 書本

例句

· Many children are told to bury their noses in their books.
許多小孩被要求要埋頭好好讀書。

· Still many people hope that traditional books will not be replaced by e-reading.
仍然有許多人希望傳統的書本不要被電子閱讀取代。

 訂飛機等座位或訂旅館等房間；指警方對嫌犯的登記做為指控之用（to press charge against someone, generally by the police）

例句

· Mr. Chen has booked（或 made） a reservation at a hotel.
陳先生訂了旅館房間。

· Yesterday he booked a flight to Taiwan.
昨天他訂好到台灣的飛機。

· The flight was booked to full capacity.
飛機的訂座都滿了。

· The police have booked this suspect for murder.
警察逮捕這位謀殺嫌犯。

· The police booked him for drunken driving.
警察控他酒後駕車。

bow

◀)) 008

 鞠躬 [baʊ]

例句

· The man bows for (to) the queen.
這位男士向皇后鞠躬。

名詞 「蝶形結」或「彩結」[bo];「弓」[bo];「船頭」[baʊ]

例句

· People always place a bow on the gift.
人們常常在禮物上放個彩結。

· He used a bow to shoot an arrow.
他拉弓射箭。

· The bow of the ship was being hit by the strong waves.
船頭被大浪沖激。

box

🔊 009

名詞 箱;盒;包廂（觀眾）

例句

· Some people can eat a whole box of candy.
有些人可以吃下一整盒的糖果。

· The VIPs in their boxes applauded the singer.
包廂內的名流向歌唱者鼓掌。（VIP = very important person）

動詞 打耳光

例句

· When he gets mad, he boxes his son's ears.
他生氣時，就打兒子的耳光。

· To box a child's ears may have a lasting effect.
打孩子的耳光，可能有長遠的影響。

- He felt bad to have boxed his wife's ears during the fight.
  他為吵架時打太太的耳光而感到難過。

- He learned to box the compass.
  他學習操作羅盤針方向。（ to box the compass 是特別的一種用法）

bridge

名詞 橋樑；橋牌

例句

- A new bridge will soon be built across the river.
  過河的新橋即將建造。

- Some people enjoy playing bridge during the weekend.
  有些人喜歡在週末打橋牌。

動詞 連接或溝通（ to connect ）

例句

- My purpose of writing articles is to bridge the cultural differences between Chinese and Americans.
  我寫文章的目的是要消除中美人民文化的分歧。

- The parents are trying to bridge the generation gap with their children.
  父母都在設法彌合與兒女的代溝。

- Before divorce, parents should bridge their differences.
  離婚前，父母應該彌補分歧。

can

 011

 能;能夠

例句

· Can (Could) you help me in the lab?
你能在實驗室幫我忙嗎？
（lab = laboratory）

動詞 解雇;指把水果、蔬菜等裝入罐內或瓶內,密封後而貯存之。
（動詞時態: can, canned, canning）

例句

· John was canned from the job.
John 被解雇了（= fired）。

· The woman canned the fruits.
婦人把水果貯存於罐中。

· She tried to can more vegetables.
她想裝更多的蔬菜。

名詞 罐

例句

· I bought a can of peas at the store.
我從店裡買了一個豆子的罐頭。

既然 can 可當做助動詞 (*a.v.*),動詞 (*v.*) 和名詞 (*n.*),所以有人好玩地說:
A canner can (*a.v.*) can (*v.*) anything that he can. (*a.v.*)
或 A canner can (*a.v.*) can (*v.*) a can (*n.*), can't (*a.v.*) he?
（canner 是指裝製罐頭的人）

cap

🔊 012

 名詞 便帽

例句

· When a man enters the room, he usually takes off his cap.
男士進屋時，通常要脫下帽子。

· When you graduate from a 4-year college, you wear a cap and gown.
當你從四年制的大學畢業時，你要戴上學士帽和穿上學士袍。

動詞 限額、約束或制止（to limit something）

例句

· It is said that the Chinese government will cap the spending for military purposes.
據說中國政府將限制軍事的開支。

· The new law has capped the crabbing season in our area.
新法令限制了本地區捕蟹的季節。（即不准隨時捕蟹）

· Our school will cap the white student enrollment to promote its diversity programs.
本校為了提高種族的多元性，而限制白人學生的入學率。

carpet

 🔊 013

 地毯

例句

- Most American people have wall-to-wall carpet at home.
  大部分老美家裡的全部地板都舖滿地毯。

- His 20-year-old carpet needs to be replaced.
  他二十年的舊地毯需要更換。

動詞 覆蓋（to cover something）

例句

- The flower girls carpeted the floor with rose petals before the bride's entrance.
  新娘進來前，花童以玫瑰花瓣撒滿了地板。

- Many fans continued to carpet the movie star's grave with a variety of flowers.
  許多影迷持續在明星的墓前放滿各式各樣的花。

- During the winter time, my roof is carpeted with white snow.
  冬天時我家的屋頂被白雪覆蓋。

catch

🔊 014

 捉住、捕獲、鉤住

例句

· How many fish did you catch yesterday?
昨天你捕了幾條魚？

· Her new dress caught on a nail.
她的新衣被釘子鉤住。

 大量的捕獲物、圈套；問題（困難）

例句

· Mr. A is not sure of a good catch today.
A 先生沒有把握今天能捕到大量的魚。

· There must be a catch in his long-term plan.
他的長期計畫中肯定有花樣。

· There is a catch for her (in) finding a "Mr. Right."
她要找位「如意郎君」有問題（困難）。（catch = problem or difficulty）

 微妙的、難以捉摸的

例句

· The teacher likes to give some catch questions on the test.
老師喜歡出些難以捉摸的考題。（catch = tricky）

cement

 水泥

例句

· We hope all the backroads in China are one day paved with cement.
盼望有一天在中國的所有小路，都是水泥鋪成的。
註：backroad 指鄉下的小路，不是「後面的路」。

 加強、鞏固（動詞時態：cemented, cementing）

例句

· Spending more time together and understanding each other may cement their friendship.
常在一起和彼此了解，可以鞏固友誼。

· The U.S. and China need to cement their foreign relations.
中美兩國需要加強它們的外交關係。

· Over the past few years, the economic ties between Taiwan and China have been cemented.
過去幾年來，台灣與大陸間的經貿已經加強。

· If Chinese people want to earn more respect from other countries, they should cement their cooperation and unity among themselves.
假如中國人要獲得其他國家的尊重，那麼他們之間必須合作和團結。

· To avoid racial prejudice, Americans have been cementing relations among the races.
為了避免種族偏見，美國人已在加強族群間的關係。

chair

 016

 椅子；會議的主席（= chairman 或 chairwoman = chairperson）

例句

· There is a cast-iron chair on his porch.
在他陽台上有張鐵製的椅子。

· The committee chair called the meeting to order.
委員會主席宣布開會。

動詞 擔任會議的主席（to be a chairperson）

例句

· He has chaired a committee on international affairs.
他擔任國際事務委員會的主席。

· One of my colleagues loves to chair several sub-committees on campus.
我的一位同事喜歡擔任學校裡幾個分會的主持人。

· She will chair the math department next semester.
下學期她將擔任數學系系主任。

channel

 017

 名詞 途徑或路線

例句

· International conflicts should be solved through diplomatic channels.
國際上的衝突應藉外交途徑解決。

· Through normal channels, it takes many months for an immigrant to get a visa.
循正常管道,要花幾個月才能取得移民簽證。

· There should be a better channel of communication between the U.S. and China.
中美兩國該有較好的溝通管道。

 動詞 集中;引導或貫注

例句

· Mr. A tries to channel his time into charity work.
A 先生把他的時間集中在慈善工作上。

· Many organizations channel health information to us.
許多機關為我們傳遞健康訊息。

· More research funds will be channeled in finding better ways to cure cancer.
為了找到較好的治癌方法,將調撥更多的研究資金。

· By channeling dialogue, the relationship between Taiwan and China can be improved.
透過對話渠道,台灣與中國的關係將會改善。

club

🔊 018

名詞　俱樂部；高爾夫球棒

例句

· Mr. A joined the chess club last week.
上週 A 先生參加象棋俱樂部。

· Golfers always carry a set of clubs.
高爾夫運動員經常帶著一套球桿。

動詞　用棍棒打人（to beat someone with a stick）

例句

· The security officer should not club any suspect who does not resist arrest.
安全人員對任何沒有拒捕的嫌犯不該用棒毆打。

· I saw the police clubbing a suspected robber.
我看到警察用棒子打擊搶劫嫌疑犯。

· When John insulted Mary, he clubbed her on the arm.
當 John 侮辱 Mary 時，他用棒子打她的手臂。

coed

🔊 019

形容詞　如果後面有其他字眼，是指「男女合校」（coed 這個字，實際上就是 coeducational 的縮寫）

例句

· A girl was residing in a coed dormitory.
一位女生住在男女合住的學生宿舍。

如果 coed 後面沒有其他字眼,則指「大學的女生」。

例句

· A coed was murdered at the mall last year.
去年一位大學女生在採購中心遇害。

 condition ◀)) 020

 條件

例句

· There shouldn't be conditions attached to a marriage.
婚姻不該有附帶條件。

動詞 訓練某人做某事(to train someone to do something)(後
面多半跟反身代名詞 oneself)(動詞時態是:conditioned
conditioning)

例句

· Many workers have been conditioned to say "Yes" to the boss.
許多工人被訓練老闆說「是」的習慣。

· They are trying to condition themselves to the extremely cold
weather.
他們訓練自己適應嚴寒的天氣。

· I will condition myself to face my writing difficulty.
我要訓練自己面對寫作的困難。

· The widow has conditioned herself to live alone.
寡婦已適應自己獨居的生活。

corner

◀) 021

 名詞 角落或壁角

例句

- The store is located at the corner.
  店舖就在那角落。

- I will meet you on (at) the corner of 2nd and 5th Streets.
  我在第二街和第五街的角落與你碰面。

 動詞 將某人逼入困境或令人無地自容（to put someone in a bad spot）

例句

- Don't try to corner your spouse.
  不可讓你的另一半走入困境。

- He has been cornered by his best friend.
  他的好友使他走投無路。

- She has cornered her boyfriend.
  她把男友逼入困境。

- Finally, the escaped criminal was cornered.
  那逃犯終於陷入困境。

cushion

 022

名詞 坐墊

例句

· We put several cushions on our sofa.
我們在沙發上放幾個靠墊。

· The woman knelt (down) on a cushion to pray.
這女子跪在墊子上祈禱。

動詞 緩和或降低對某事的撞擊或震動（to soften or decrease impact of something）

例句

· He cushions his transition into retirement by referring to himself as a lame duck.
他為了減少衝擊，在退休過程的轉移中，自稱為跛腳鴨。

· Taiwan has been cushioning its economic downfall by opening up a trade relation with China.
台灣為了緩和經濟的下降而與中國大陸開放貿易關係。

· Nothing can cushion the sorrow of her mother's death.
什麼都不能減輕她對母親去世的悲傷。

desert

🔊 023

 沙漠 [ˈdɛzɚt]（不可與 dessert「飯後甜點」弄錯）

例句

· Many people living in the desert will have a hard time finding water.
在沙漠生活的人，很難找到水。

 放棄 [dɪˈzɝt]

例句

· As she is on diet, she likes to desert her dessert every day.
她因為節食，所以每天不吃甜點。

· The soldier decided to desert his dessert in the desert.
士兵在沙漠裡放棄他的甜點。

discriminating

🔊 024

名詞 discrimination：「偏見」或「歧視」

例句

· Many people are fighting against racial discrimination in the U.S.
在美國許多人反對種族歧視。

動詞 discriminate：歧視（後面多跟 against）

例句

· Don't discriminate against the handicapped people.
不要對殘疾者有偏見。

· The company is discriminating against him because of nationality.
由於不同國籍，公司對他有偏見。（進行式）

· Discriminating against minorities is illegal.
歧視少數民族是違法的。（動名詞）

 形容詞 discriminating：「有鑑賞能力」，「有選擇好壞的能力」
（good taster, selective）（多半用在藝術或音樂方面）

例句

· Mrs. Lin has a discriminating taste in art and music.
林太太對藝術和音樂有很高的鑑賞能力。

· Your selection of living room furniture is quite discriminating.
你對客廳家具的選擇是很有品味的。

· Be discriminating but honest.
要有選擇的能力，但也要誠實。
（這裡的 discriminating 有 choosy 的意思）

distance

 025

 距離；路程

例句

· Personally speaking, I don't enjoy long-distance flights or drives.
就我個人來說，我不愛長途旅行或開車。

· It would be difficult for Mr. A to keep his distance from his ex-girlfriend.
A 先生與從前的女友很難保持疏遠。

動詞 指冷淡、疏遠或保持與某人的距離（to keep yourself a distance from someone）

例句

· It is difficult for him to distance himself from her.
他要與她疏遠可不容易。

· The politicians will distance themselves from the controversial issues.
政客們想要與爭論性的問題保持距離。

· The parents advise their daughter to distance herself from her boyfriend.
父母勸告女兒要與男友保持距離。

doctor

 名詞　醫生、大夫（= physician）

例句

· If you don't feel well, you have to see a doctor.
假如你不舒服，你就要看醫生。

· In the US, you will have to make an appointment with a doctor.
在美國，你必須與醫生預約。

 動詞　用藥治病或放藥物在飲料裡（to give medical treatment; or to put drug in one's drink）

例句

· Someone tried to doctor her drink at the party.
宴會時，有人想把毒品放在她的飲料裡。（多指迷幻藥）
（= to put some drug in her drink）

· The mother was trying to doctor her children by using over-the-counter medication.
這位母親想買成藥給她孩子吃。

但是 to doctor the number = to cook the book 是做假帳（to make something fraudulent or false）

· He tried to doctor the number before tax time.
他在報稅前設法做假帳。

· People who doctor the numbers may end up in jail one day.
做假帳的人，有一天會坐牢的。
（註：也有人用 to doctor the book）

does

◄)) 027

 doe「母鹿」[do]（= female deer）如果複數加 s，就變成 does

例句

· The does were standing together in the forest.
在森林裡母鹿站在一起。

動詞 do 用在第三人稱，單數，現在式，也要加 es，形成 does [dʌz]

例句

· The student does his homework every day.
學生每天做他的功課。

· The buck does funny things when the does are present.
當母鹿出現時，公鹿就會做出一些有趣的動作。
（buck 是公鹿 = male deer）

dog

◄)) 028

 狗

例句

· Some people treat their dog(s) better than human being(s).
有些人對待狗比對待人還好。

· To keep a dog seems to be time and money consuming.
養狗似乎是費時費錢的差事。

困擾某人或某事（to bother someone or something）；
跟隨（像狗跟隨主人一樣）

例句

· He was dogged wherever he went.
他不管到那裡，總被打擾。

· Human rights protesters tried to dog Mr. Jiang's official visit to England.
人權份子打擾江先生對英國的國事訪問。

· The death of her husband has dogged her for months.
她老公的去世，使她難過數個月。

· U.S.-China relations have been dogged by the Taiwan issue for years.
中美關係受到台灣問題多年的困擾。

· You don't have to dog your father's footsteps.
你不必步你父親的後塵。（to dog = to follow）

· The Taiwan issue has been dogging the leaders of the U.S. and China for decades.
數十年來，台灣問題一直跟隨著中美兩國的領袖。

dove

◀)) 029

 指「鴿子」（通常是和平的象徵）[dʌv]

例句

· The couple released a dove at their wedding.
這對夫婦在婚禮上釋放一隻和平鴿。

動詞 dive「潛入」的過去式及過去分詞也是 dove [dov]

例句

· The swimmer dove from the platform.
游泳者從跳水台上潛入水裡。

· When shot at, the dove dove into the bushes.
= When the hunter shot at the dove, it dove into the bushes for safety.
當射手瞄準時，鴿子潛進叢林。

down

◀)) 030

 失意；鳥類的軟毛

例句

· Every life has its ups and downs.
生命中都有得意和失意的時候。

· Many down comforters were on sale last week.
許多鴨絨被上週大減價。（down = goose down）

28

動詞 擊落、墜落（多半指飛機）

例句

· Engine trouble downed the aircraft.
引擎的毛病，導致飛機墜落。

· The U.S. pilots have downed several enemy jets in the war.
在戰場美國飛行員擊落數架敵人的飛機。

形容詞 下降；不高興

例句

· The business was down ten percent from last year.
生意比去年下降 10%。

· Mr. A was feeling a little bit down today.
A 先生今天有點悶悶不樂。

副詞 往下

例句

· The man fell down and injured his foot.
這男士跌下來，傷了他的腳。

· You may feel better if you lie down for a while.
你去躺一會，也許會好些。

介詞 沿著或那邊

例句

· The truck was parked down the street.
卡車停在馬路的那邊。

· The lady walked down the hall to the elevator.
婦女沿著走廊向電梯走去。
（down the street 和 down the hall 都成為介詞片語，當副詞用，
修飾動詞 parked 和 walked）

duck

◀) 031

名詞 鴨子

例句

· Many Chinese love roast Beijing duck.
許多中國人愛吃北京烤鴨。

· The boy keeps a duck as his pet in his backyard.
這男孩在他的後院養了隻鴨子當寵物。

動詞 躲藏（to hide）

例句

· Be sure to duck (yourself) under a safe place if necessary.
必要時你要躲在安全的地方。

· When danger occurs, the first thing we need to do is to duck.
當危險發生時，第一件事我們要做的就是躲藏起來。

engineer

◀)) 032

名詞 工程師、技師

例句

· Mr. Wang pushed his son to become a good engineer.
王先生逼他兒子當個好工程師。

動詞 設計或策劃

例句

· Mr. A was the one who engineered the project from start to finish.
這個計畫從頭到尾都是 A 先生設計的。

· The suspect tried to engineer a plot to kill his boss.
嫌犯密謀殺害他的老闆。（to engineer= to plan）

· Some professors engineer their courses differently.
有些教授以不同方式，設計他們的課程。（engineer = design）

· Mr. A is outstanding to have engineered such a pretty bridge.
A 先生很棒，設計這座漂亮的橋。

fair

◀)) 033

名詞 商展會

例句

· Our state fair will be held here next month.
下個月我們州政府的商展會將在此地舉行。

形容詞　美麗的；公平的

例句

· All criminals should be given fair trials.
所有罪犯應該得到公正的審判。

· A fair lady went to the county fair yesterday.
一位漂亮的女士昨天參觀縣裡的商展會。

fasting

🔊 034

 形容詞 / 副詞　fast：快、迅速

例句

· He runs really fast.（副詞）
= He is a fast runner.（形容詞）
他跑得很快。

· Generally, Americans speak English fast.（副詞）
一般而言，美國人講英文的速度很快。

· He gave me a fast response.（形容詞）
他給我一個很快的回答。

動詞　fast：為了某種原因而「禁食」或「忌食」（not to eat）
（一般指健康方面），

例句

· The nurse told me to fast ten hours before the blood test.
護士告訴我在抽血檢查前十小時不能吃東西。（多半可以喝水）

· She is fasting because she wants to lose weight.
由於她想減輕體重所以不吃東西。（只喝水份）

fasting：變瘦、苗條（fasting = thin）

例句

· Parents advise girls not to be fasting females.
父母勸告女孩不要成為太瘦的女性。

 fare　◀》035

名詞　車票、船票、飛機票等

例句

· The airline fare to Taiwan will probably be raised.
飛台灣的機票也許會漲價。

· The daughter will pay the cruise ship fare for her parents.
女兒要為她的父母購買海上航遊的船票。

動詞　過活、進展或處境（to get along or to turn out）

例句

· How do you fare? = How are you doing?

· I fare very well. = I am doing (feeling) well.

· How did you fare on your exam?（考得怎樣？）

· I fared very well on my exam.（考得不錯。）

· Taiwan's economy is faring worse than before.
台灣經濟不如過去。

· If he gets caught for shoplifting, he may fare a punishment.
如果他偷竊被捕，將會受到處分。

fashion

 036

 方式，樣子

例句

· Rich people love to live in a lavish fashion.
富人喜歡採取浪費的生活方式。（= style）

動詞 形成（to make）（動詞時態是：fashioned, fashioning）

例句

· He writes many newspaper articles, trying to fashion public opinion.
他在報上寫了許多文章，想要形成大眾的意見。（= to make）

· Mr. A fashioned a job that would give him a more flexible schedule.
A 先生把工作時間變成較有彈性。

· He has fashioned his 40-year life experience into a book.
他把 40 年的生活經驗，集成一本書。

father

 037

名詞 父親

例句

· In order to be a responsible father, you should set good examples.
為了做個負責的父親，你要樹立好的榜樣。

· Many politicians have lived in the shadow of their famous father.
許多政客生活在他們父親的盛名之下。

 指父方而言生孩子（to beget a child）

例句

· He has fathered two children before his remarriage.
他再婚前生了兩個孩子。

· Hopefully, Mr. Chen is going to father a child soon.
但願陳先生很快能當爸爸。

注意：如果以母方來說，就是：

She bore him two children.
她為他生了兩個孩子。
或 She has born two children.
（動詞時態是：bear, bore, born）
或 She bore a son. 也就是 He begot a son.
（動詞時態是：beget, begot, begot 或 begotten）
A son was born by her. 也就是：A son was begotten by him.
所以 to father a child，也就是 to beget a child
（也可用任何動詞時態）

 fault 🔊 038

 缺點、過錯

例句

· Mr. A committed a serious fault and had to step down from his position.
A 先生犯了嚴重過錯，必須引咎辭職。

· According to the police, this car accident was the driver's fault.
根據警察的說法，這起車禍是司機的錯。

動詞 挑剔或批評

例句

· Many scholars tend to fault others easily.
許多學者有輕易挑剔他人的傾向。

· Some people faulted the mayor for failing to take a tough stand.
有些人批評市長沒有採取強硬的立場。

· No one is perfect; we should not try to fault others all the time.
沒有人是十全十美的；我們不該常常批評別人。

field

◀)) 039

名詞 場地

例句

· Children are playing baseball in the field.
孩子在場地上打棒球。

動詞 供給（to supply）（動詞時態是：fielded, fielding）

例句

· Our school hopes to field a competitive team for the upcoming football season.
學校希望派一支有競爭性的球隊參加即將來臨的足球季。
（= to supply a team, or to put a team on the field）

· For 2008, the Democrats would field a set of strong candidates
for president.
2008 年，民主黨人士將推出一組堅強的總統候選人。

 另外由於 field 這個字，本是來自棒球賽，所以常常是接到球
與守住球的意思

例句

· The player was unable to field the ball cleanly.
球員不能熟練的接球。（也就是接到球，又掉下來，不能守住球。
cleanly 是靈巧的，熟練的）

· Fielding / To field the ball is very important (to a player).
接到球，守住球（不會再掉下去），對球員是很重要的。
（catch the ball without dropping）

· The president has to field many questions from the reporters.
總統答覆記者們提出的許多問題。
（記者把問題丟給總統，總統 catch 後，再應付和答覆。）

fishing

◀)) 040

----

 fish：魚（fish 與 fishes 意義上有不同）

例句

· I caught a lot of fish.
我釣到很多魚。（這裡的 fish 是指一般性的魚，沒有單複數之分，
所以不加 es。）

· I have caught many fishes.
我釣到很多魚。（這裡的 fishes 是指許多不同種類的魚）

fish：1. 釣魚；2. 尋求、設法得到（多半指誇獎方面）（to search for or try to obtain）

例句

· I went fishing. = I went to fish.
我去釣魚。

· Are you fishing in the ocean?
你在海邊釣魚嗎？

· Fishing is one of his hobbies.
釣魚是他的一項嗜好。

· Are you fishing for my compliments?
你想得到我的誇獎嗎？

· She has been fishing (has fished) for praise from her boss for years.
她多年來一直就盼望得到上司的稱讚。
（用現在完成進行式 has been fishing 強調盼望「還在繼續」，而現在完成式 has fished 意味盼望也許「已經停止」）

· Mr. Chang is fishing for a new girl friend.
張先生想找一位新女友。

 flag

 041

 旗幟

例句

· All citizens will respect their national flag.
所有人民都尊敬國旗。

· To honor its president's death, a nation will lower flags to half staff.
全國為總統逝世而降半旗致哀。

 指打旗號或做手勢，表示傳達訊息（to give signal for communication）

例句

· When my car broke down, I flagged a police car.
當我汽車出毛病，我打信號招來一輛警車。
或 A police car appeared and I flagged it down.
一部警車出現，我招手請它停下。

· The beach life-guards usually flag one another for communication.
海灘救生員通常用旗號傳達訊息。

floor

 042

 地板

例句

· Many Americans prefer hard-wood floor for their living room.
許多老美的客廳喜歡硬木的地板。

· This newly-built library has four floors.
這棟新蓋圖書館有四層樓。

動詞 踩足汽車的油門踏板，加速開車（to press accelerator of a car to the floor in order to speed up）；使人驚訝（to astonish someone）

例句

· As soon as I saw his gun, I floored my car.
　一旦看到他有槍，我立即加速開車。

· When you see a police car, don't floor it.
　當你看到警車時，別開快車。

· He floored his car in order to beat the traffic during the rush hours.
　他開快車是想避免交通擁擠時間。

· He floored me when he said he had an affair with his secretary.
　他說與他的祕書有染，令我驚訝。

 fly ◀) 043

名詞 指「蒼蠅」；也指「褲子前面的拉鍊」

例句

· Mr. Chen was trying to kill a fly but accidentally burst his fly.
　陳先生打蒼蠅時，褲子前面的拉鍊突然裂開。

· His fly burst open during the meeting.
　他開會時褲子的拉鍊裂開。

· The crazy man unzipped his fly on purpose.
　這位瘋狂的男子故意不拉上褲子的拉鍊。
　（動詞 zip 是「拉上拉鍊」的意思，過去式及過去分詞是 zipped）
　（unzip 就是「拉不上拉鍊」）

foot

名詞 腳;底部;英尺

例句

· My feet are sore after walking ten miles.
走了 10 哩路,我的腳痠痛了。

· There is a temple at the foot of a hill.
在山丘底下有座廟宇。

· This six-foot tall woman plays basketball well.
這位 6 呎高的女子,籃球打得不錯。

動詞 付帳

例句

· His father foots his electricity bill every month.
他父親每月付電費。

· In Chinese society, the man generally foots the bill for dating expenses.
在中國社會裡與女友約會,通常是男人付帳。

· Through his generosity, Mr. A has footed the phone bill for his roommate.
A 先生很慷慨地為室友付電話費。

fuel

 045

名詞 燃料

_例句_

· The U.S. Is seeking more resources for its fuel.
美國正在尋求更多燃料的資源。

動詞 增加或刺激（to increase or to stimulate）（動詞時態是：
fueled, fueling）

_例句_

· He told his wife that he had an affair in order to fuel her jealousy.
他告訴太座他有外遇，為了增加她的嫉妒。（= to increase）

· The inflation has been fueled by the military spending.
軍事上的開支，對通貨膨脹是火上加油。
（= to put fuel on the fire）

· While discussing this controversial issue, he is fueling her anger.
談到爭議性的問題時，他添加了她的憤怒。

· Racial discrimination sometimes will fuel civil unrest.
種族歧視，有時會添加國內的不安。

· Our new students create a market that fuels our economy.
新來的學生，創造一個刺激我們經濟的市場。（= to stimulate）

gift

 046

名詞 禮物或天賦、天才

例句

· Mr. A made a gift of ten thousand dollars to the school.
A 先生贈給學校 1 萬元。

· Many politicians have the gift of speaking well.
許多政客有口才。（**gift** 指天賦 = talent，故 politicians 雖是複數，但 **gift** 仍用單數）

動詞 贈送

例句

· To gift your boss with a new book on Christmas is not bribery.
聖誕節贈送老闆一本新書，不是賄賂。

· Mr. B gifted his wife with heart-shaped diamond earrings.
B 先生送給太座心型的鑽石耳環。

形容詞 gifted 當形容詞：有天分的、有天賦的

例句

· Generally speaking, Americans do not overpraise the gifted children in public.
一般而言，老美不像老中那樣，愛在大眾面前，誇耀資優孩子。

· John has been gifted in mathematics since he was three.
John 從 3 歲起，就有數學天賦。

grandfather ◀)) 047

名詞 祖父

例句

· My grandfather was a pretty well-known scholar in my native town.
  我祖父在我老家是為頗具盛名的學者。

· Generally speaking, grandmothers will outlive grandfathers.
  一般而言,祖母比祖父長壽。

動詞 保護(免受限制)或保持現狀(to protect or to keep the same status)。

例句

· Our current employees will be grandfathered under the existing health insurance.
  在現有的健保制度下,目前員工受到保護。

· Everybody would like to grandfather this regulation as is.
  對於這個規定每個人都想保持原狀。

· The new staff members cannot be grandfathered into the old pension system.
  新進職員不受過去養老金制度的保護。

ground

◀)) 048

 土地；根據或基礎

例句

- During the hot argument, he threw a cup to the ground.
  在激烈的爭吵中，他把杯子摔在地上。

- Adultery can be used as a ground for divorce.
  通姦可作為離婚的理由。

- He has good grounds for what he is doing.
  他的行為很有根據。

 打好基礎；禁止

例句

- Many Chinese students are well grounded in math.
  許多中國學生的數學基礎打得很好。

- The bad weather has grounded many flights / planes.
  天氣不好使許多飛機停飛。

- The boy has been grounded for his misconduct.
  這男孩因行為不良而被禁足。

heat

◀)) 049

 熱度、高溫或波動

例句

- Some people speak with lots of heat.
  有些人說話很激動。（= high emotion or anger）

- If you can't stand the heat, stay out of the kitchen.
  要是你受不了熱，就別待在廚房裡。（這是 Harry Truman 的名言，意指如果缺乏膽量、精力或容忍強烈批評的勇氣，就不要謀求總統職位）

動詞 加熱、使激動或使憤怒

例句

- Dr. Wang's arrogance has heated us beyond tolerance.
  王醫師的傲慢，使我們難以忍受。

- The presidential campaign is heating up in its final days.
  總統競選活動在最後幾天，趨於白熱化。

形容詞 heated 當形容詞：激烈的意思

例句

- Taiwan's legislators had many heated debates at its meetings.
  台灣立委開會時，有多次激烈的辯論。

- The husband and wife always have a heated argument over parenting.
  他們夫妻為管教孩子而激烈爭吵。

house

🔊 050

名詞 房屋

例句

- A beautiful house could be a target for a break-in.
  漂亮的房子，可能是盜竊的目標。

· Actually, a house is to live in; not for show.
其實房子是供人住的，不是作為炫燿用的。

 供給住所（to provide shelter）

例句

· The farmer has housed the horse in the barn.
農夫讓馬住在馬房裡。

· The detention center will house ten thousand illegal immigrants.
監禁中心將供給一萬名違法移民居住。

· I would be glad to house you for the weekend.
我很高興週末能提供你住所。

husband

  ◀)) 051

名詞 丈夫

例句

· As a nice husband, John takes good care of his better half.
John 是位好老公，細心照顧他的另一半。

動詞 省錢；節約

例句

· The president of Taiwan has husbanded its national budget.
台灣總統節省國家的預算。

- It would be a good idea for Americans to husband natural resources.
美國人最好能節約使用自然資源。

- Husbanding your spending will add to your nest-egg.
節省開支能增加你將來的儲備金。（nest-egg 多指退休後能用的存款）

ice

🔊 052

名詞 冰或冰塊

例句

- The boy was carefully walking on the ice.
這男孩在冰上小心行走。

- He bought a bag of ice for camping.
他為露營而買一袋冰塊。

動詞 指比賽中勝過對方（to win or to beat in competition）（多指體育競賽）

例句

- Stanford University has iced the University of Maryland in a football game.
史大足球賽大勝馬大。

- Our school ices all the competitions in basketball.
本校籃球比賽屢戰屢勝。

- The swimming team members want to ice their rivals.
游泳隊的成員，想要勝過對手。

ill

◀)) 053

 指「生病」，但 ill 與 afford 連用時，意思是「付不起」。

· This poor man was ill and could ill afford to buy medicine.
這位生病的窮人付不起醫藥費。（ill = not）

· It is a vital publication and we can ill afford to lose.
這是一份重要的刊物；我們不能失去它。

 ill：有「壞話」的意思

例句

· Don't speak ill of others.
不要說別人壞話。

invalid

◀)) 054

形容詞 失效的 [ɪnˈvælɪd]

例句

· His driver's license is invalid.
他的駕駛執照已經失效。

名詞 指「殘障者」（invalid 當「殘障者」解，複數可加 s）[ˈɪnvəlɪd]

例句

- The invalid needs all kinds of health insurance.
  殘障者需要各種的健康保險。

- The insurance was invalid for the invalid.
  這個保險對殘障者是無效的。

invaluable

🔊 055

名詞 value：意思是「價值」

例句

- This property has great value.
  這房地產有很高的價值。

形容詞 valuable：意思是「寶貴的」、「值錢的」

例句

- Your valuable advice is highly appreciated.
  你的寶貴忠言是令人感佩的。

名詞 valuable：「貴重物品」的意思

例句

- He has many valuables in his safe.
  他在保險箱裡有很多值錢的東西。

形容詞 invaluable：不是「不貴重」，反而是「非常貴重」（= very valuable or indispensable）這種特別用法，多半是在誇獎一個人的服務成績。

例句

· Mr. Lee has rendered invaluable services to our school for many years.
多年來李先生對本校做出寶貴的服務。

· As an invaluable employee of this company, he received an achievement award yesterday.
由於他是本公司難得的一員，他昨天接受一項工作成就獎。

inviting

◀)) 056

動詞 invite：邀請（invitation 是名詞）

例句

· Did you invite her to the dinner last night?
你昨晚有請她吃飯嗎？

· I am inviting some friends to a party tomorrow.
明天我要請些朋友來聚會。（進行式）

= I will invite some friends...（因為老外常把現在進行式與未來式互用）

· Inviting friends for dinner could be enjoyable.
請朋友吃飯是很愉快的。（動名詞）

51

形容詞 inviting：「吸引人的」，「漂亮的」，「好看的」
（attractive, good-looking or pleasant）

例句

· The most inviting building on our campus is the student recreation center.
我們校園裡最吸引人的建築物就是學生活動中心。

· Big windows allow passersby to see the inviting interior decoration.
大的櫥窗可以讓行人看到漂亮的內部裝飾。
（passerby 是單數，複數是 passersby）

· She has an inviting personality.
她有令人感到愉快的品格。

journey

◀)) 057

名詞 行程或旅行

例句

· Last week Mr. A made a journey around the world.
上週 A 先生環遊世界。

動詞 去旅行（to travel）；經歷過（動詞時態：journeyed, journeying）

例句

· Mr. Wang is going to journey to Hong Kong soon.
王先生即將去香港旅行。

· Journeying (To journey) to Russia would be a great experience for me.
去蘇聯旅行，對我是件很大的體驗。

· The couple have journeyed together for twenty years.
這對夫婦一起生活了 20 年。

· I have journeyed far and wide during my forty years in America.
在美國，我有 40 年廣泛的閱歷。

lead

 058

 「帶領」的意思 [lid]

例句

· He will lead the swimming team for our school.
他將代表本校帶領游泳隊。

 領先 [lid]；又指「鉛」 [lɛd]

例句

· He could lead if he would get the lead out.
他的動作能敏捷快速，他就能更有效的領隊。

也就是說：

· He could lead the group more efficiently if he would get the lead out of his feet.（to get the lead out = to speed up）

· Don't be a lead foot driver.
不要開快車。（lead foot 指像鉛那麼重的腳，油門就會踩得重，車子就跑太快了）

level

◄)) 059

 水準或水平

 例句

· China has to catch up with the military advanced level in the world.
中國要趕上世界軍事的高水平。

· The U.S. and China will hold a conference at the ministerial level.
中美將舉行一次部長級的會議。

 弄平或摧毀

例句

· The storm leveled many trees in the city.
風暴把城內許多樹木颳倒。

· The building will be leveled next week.
下星期樓房將被鏟平。

· The bulldozer will level the road before paving.
在鋪路前，推土機將把路鏟平。

形容詞 平坦的、水平差不多的意思

例句

· Most street are pretty level.
大部分的馬路是很平坦的。

· These two students are almost level in chemistry.
這兩位學生化學的水平差不多。

light

形容詞 緩和的；容易消化的；有偷竊習慣的；少量的；安靜的

例句

· The doctor advised him to take very light exercise.
醫生勸他做些緩和運動。（= little）

· Most people need only a light lunch.
多半人只吃清淡容易消化的午餐（= digestible）

· The child has light fingers. = The child is light fingered.
這孩子有偷竊的惡習。（= stealing habit）

· The apple crop is light this year.
今年蘋果的收成欠佳。（= not bountiful）

· The cat is light on its feet.
貓走路是很安靜的。（= very quiet）

名詞 火；燈

例句

· He struck a match for a light.
他擦火柴點火。（= fire）（動詞時態：strike, struck, struck (stricken)）

· There is only a light in his room.
他房間只有一盞燈。（= lamp light）

動 詞 點火、開火；使容光煥發

 例句

· Light the oven before you put the cookies in.
　先開烤箱，再放進餅乾。（ light = turn on the heat ）

· Her face was lighted (lit) by her smile.
　她的微笑使她容光煥發。（動詞時態：light, lit, lit 或 lighted, lighted ）

live

◀)) 061

 動 詞 生存，但在第三人稱，單數，現在式，後面要加 s，變成 lives。

例句

· He lives a very happy life.
　他活得很痛快。

名 詞 life 的多數，也是 lives

例句

· The lives of my family members are as good as yours.
　我家人的生活與你的家人一樣好。

· The significance of our lives lives in our hearts.
　我們生命的意味是活在我們的心裡。
　（第一個 lives 是 life 的複數；第二個 lives 是動詞 live 第三人稱單數現在式後面加 s ）

loose

 062

形容詞 放蕩的;亂花錢的;鬆動的

例句

- His wife is loose with her money.
  他的太太亂花錢。(= big spender)

- Mr. Lin is loose with his children.
  林先生對他的孩子管教很鬆。(= not strict)

- The screw is loose.
  螺絲鬆動了。

- She is loose.
  她的行為放蕩。或(她為人隨和。)

- The woman is loose and has a loose lip.
  這個女人行為放蕩,同時信口亂說話。(loose lip 指說話不小心)

man

 063

名詞 男人,不用冠詞時指人類

例句

- Be a man and face your own problem bravely.
  做個男子漢,勇敢地面對問題。

- Man proposes and God disposes.
  謀事在人,成事在天。

動詞 操作；掌管

例句

· It will take lots of training to man a ship.
操作一艘船，需要很多訓練。

· What type of persons will you hire to man your department?
你要雇用怎樣的人員來管理你的部門？
（to man = to manage）

· By manning the production line, robots could be useful.
機器人在生產線上操作，會有幫助。

moonlight

🔊 064

名詞 月光；夜間潛逃

例句

· The moonlight on the river added some beauty to the scene.
河邊的月光，添加了美麗的景色。

· The next morning the hotel manager found that the male guest had done a moonlight flit.
翌晨旅館經理發現男性旅客夜間逃走了。（flit = flight）

動詞 夜間兼差

例句

· The 60-year-old has moonlighted as a taxi driver.
60 歲老人兼差做計程車司機。

- Many teachers would like to moonlight in order to earn extra income.
  為了掙些額外收入，許多老師兼差。

- Mr. A has a good-paying job; why is he moonlighting?
  A 先生薪水很高，他為何要兼差？

mushroom

◀))) 065

 名詞 蘑菇，或迅速發展

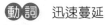 例句

- Many Chinese cook mushrooms with vegetables as a diet dish.
  許多老中用蘑菇和青菜，煮成一盤佳餚。

- Over the past years, the mushroom development of computer science seems incredible.
  近年來電腦科技迅速發展，令人難以置信。

動詞 迅速蔓延

例句

- The anti-war demonstration mushroomed into the tens of thousands.
  反戰示威，迅速蔓延到千萬人。

- After Mr. A had published several best-selling books, his popularity mushroomed.
  A 先生出了幾本暢銷書後，他的知名度蒸蒸日上。

- New buildings have mushroomed all over this area.
  這裡的新建高樓如雨後春筍般湧現。

· The fire continued to mushroom in the kitchen after fire fighters arrived.
消防隊員到達後，廚房的火勢還在繼續蔓延。

numb

🔊 066

 麻木的，但是變成形容詞比較級時又與名詞 number 的拼法相同。

例句

· After a number of injections his jaw got number.
經過多次打針後，他的下巴更加失去感覺。
（a number of = many）

· During the Japanese invasion, many Chinese minds went numb, but her mind was number.
日本侵略時，許多中國人的心志變得麻木，但她更麻木。

outstanding

🔊 067

 傑出的（excellent）；突出的（stand out）；另外「未償付的貸款」或「未清帳款」（unpaid），都叫做 outstanding（checks, bill 或 invoice 等等）

例句

· Your son is an outstanding young man.
你兒子是位很優秀的青年。

· Her red hair is outstanding in the crowd.
她的紅頭髮在人群中很突出。

- My outstanding checks have not been cashed.
  我的支票已開出去，但還未被兌現。

- The bank has one million dollars outstanding loan.
  銀行借出貸款一百萬，現在貸款人尚在償還中。

page

🔊 068

名詞 書頁；侍從

 例句

- Mr. A was lying on the sofa turning the pages of his magazine.
  A 先生躺在沙發上，翻閱他的雜誌。

- During the summer, some high school students work in the congress as pages.
  一些高中生暑假在國會裡當侍從。

動詞 呼叫某人；給人當聽差

例句

- Please page Mr. B to the front desk; someone wants to see him.
  請廣播一下，請 B 先生來服務台，有人要找他。

- I'm paging through a pictorial book.
  我在翻閱一本畫冊。

- During her internship, Mary will be paged to run errands.
  在她實習期間，Mary 會給人跑腿辦事。

- Don't worry, someone has already paged your father.
  別擔心，有人已經呼叫你的父親。

pen

◀》 069

名詞　筆；圍欄

例句

· The pen is mightier than the sword.
  筆比劍更有力量。或（筆勝於劍。）

· The animals have been kept in the pen.
  動物被關在圍欄裡。

動詞　寫作（to write）；關在欄裡（to enclose）（動詞時態是：
　　　penned, penning）

· When you have time, you may pen some articles for
  newspaper.
  你有時間，可為報紙寫稿。

· Mr. A will be penning a draft proposal tomorrow afternoon.
  A 先生明天下午草擬提案。

· Two weeks ago, Mr. B penned a contract for his company.
  兩週前，B 先生為他公司寫契約。

· For more than seven years I have penned (have been penning)
  my column for *World Journal Weekly*.
  我為《世界周刊》寫稿已七年多了。

· The dog will be penned in his backyard.
  狗關在後院的圍欄裡。（be penned = be enclosed）

· Mr. A has penned the animals in the field.
  A 先生把動物關進牧場的圍欄裡。

piece

 一片，一件

- A piece of antique furniture may cost an arm and a leg.
  一件骨董家具，也許所費不貲。
  （an arm and a leg 是俚語，很貴的意思）

動詞 組合，再復合（to combine; to put back together）（動詞時態：pieced, piecing）通常在 piece 後面加 together

- After divorce, Mrs. A has been trying to piece her life back together.
  離婚後，A 太太設法恢復她的正常生活。
  （也就是她修補過去「破碎」的日子）

- The police pieced together the evidence and solved the crime.
  警察搜集證據，解決了犯罪事件。

- Mr. Wang is piecing together his family history.
  王先生把他家庭的歷史補綴起來。

- She has pieced her story together from the gossip with her friends.
  她把與朋友的閒聊，湊成她的故事。

pitch

 071

 動詞 投擲；推銷、廣告之意

例句

· I always pitch the ball to this little boy.
我常常投球給這小孩。（= throw）

· Several merchants were trying to pitch in for a TV special in order to pitch their new products.
幾位商人設法分擔費用，為推銷他們的新產品買個電視特別節目。
（to pitch in 是指大家分擔金錢或時間去完成某事。）

· His family members will try to pitch in to build this house.
他的家人想要分擔金錢來蓋這棟房子。

· Are you going to pitch this new merchandise on TV?
你想在電視上推銷這個新商品嗎？

pocket

 072

名詞 口袋或錢袋

例句

· Mr. A has to pay his health insurance out of his own pocket.
A 先生自掏腰包付醫藥保險。

動詞 裝進腰包（多半指錢）（to put the money in the pocket）
（動詞時態是：pocketed, pocketing）

例句

· Some people are pocketing a sizable amount of taxes to finance their lavish lifestyles.
有些人把大筆的稅收，浪費在自己的生活上。

· Many selfish people pocketed charitable donations for their personal use.
許多自私的人，把慈善的捐款作為私用。

· Josh has pocketed some money under the table without other's knowing.
Josh 暗中違法得款。

· I was aiming to pocket the billiards ball.
我瞄準把撞球打進袋裡。

position

🔊 073

 位置

例句

· I am not in a position to assist you.
我不能為你效勞。（由於某種主、客觀的條件）

 安置於或位於（to locate or to place）（動詞時態是：positioned, positioning）

例句

· The fisherman will position his boat on the trailer hook very cautiously.
漁夫把他的船小心地安置在拖車的掛鉤上。（= to place）

但指人時，多半也用反身代名詞 oneself：

· Mr. A has positioned himself very well in the company.
  A 先生在公司裡，處於很好的境地。
  （也就是 A 先生機智、聰慧，一切能應付自如 savvy）

· How is this company positioning itself in the market (place)?
  這個公司在市場上處於什麼地位？

· Regarding salary, how do we position ourselves with our counter-parts?
  就薪水來說，咱們與相關人員對比，應處於什麼位子？
  （regarding 或 considering salary 也可用 salary-wise 代替，但語氣較弱）

pot

◀)) 074

 鍋子；大麻；盆

例句

· She took a pot out of the kitchen cabinet.
  她從廚房櫃子裡取出一個鍋子。

· Yesterday my wife bought pots and pans.
  昨天我太太買了一些炊具。
  （pots and pans 是廚房裡鍋盤烹飪容器等炊具的總稱）

· Many young people smoke pot.
  許多青年人吸大麻煙。
  （pot = marijuana = marihuana 大麻毒品）

· The police charged two cases in the pot bust.
  警察破獲兩個大麻煙的案件。（bust = arrest）

· Two pots of flowers stand on my table.
兩盆花放在我的桌子上。

· The pot calls the kettle black. 是一句成語
鍋子嫌罐子底黑（即五十步笑百步。）

· He has a pot-belly.
他大腹便便。（= big stomach or large belly）（指胖子）

· We will have a pot-luck dinner next Sunday.
下星期天我們有聚餐，每人帶一道菜。

※ pot-luck 是指每個人帶一份 covered dish，別人不曉得是什麼菜，也許是剩菜（leftovers 或 leftover food），吃什麼，只有靠「運氣」（luck）了。

動詞 種在盆中（動詞時態：potted, potting）

例句

· He asked her to pot the plants.
他請她把植物種在花盆中。

present

🔊》 075

動詞 給予；介紹 [prɪˈzɛnt]

例句

· I will present you our new chairperson, Mr. Lee.
我要介紹我們的新會長李先生。

名詞 禮物；現在 [`prɛzənt] （做「禮物」用時，複數可加 s ）

例句

· At present we will present a present to our boss.
現在我們將贈送一個禮物給老闆

· Since there is no time like the present, he thought it was time to present the present.
由於沒有像現在這樣的時間，他認為應該是贈送禮物的時候了。

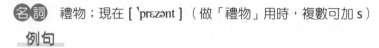

produce

◀)） 076

動詞 生產 [prə`djus]

例句

· I produce a lot of work every day.
我每天完成很多工作。

名詞 指「蔬菜果類等新鮮農產品」[`pradjus]

例句

· The farmer sells his produce in front of his house.
農夫在房子前面出售新鮮農產品。

· The farm was used to produce produce.
農場是用來生產蔬菜果類的。
（**註**：美國公路旁邊攤子所賣的蔬菜水果等，都叫 produce，單複數一樣，也不叫 farm produce，因為 produce 本身就含有 farm 的意思。不過也有人稱為 farm products ）

pride

◀)) 077

 榮譽；得意

 例句

· Mr. Ma's pride has prevented him from doing dishonest things.
馬先生的榮譽心，使他不會做出不誠實的事。

· No one should be puffed up with pride.
每個人都不該驕傲十足。（**to be puffed up** 自負）

動詞 感到得意或自豪（**to take pride in something**）（多與 oneself 或 itself 連用）

例句

· We prided ourselves on our good work.
我們為做好自己工作而得意。

· I have long prided myself on being a good teacher.
我一向以身為好教師而自豪。

· She prides herself on being a concert piano player.
她以能在演奏會彈鋼琴而得意。

· Our university has prided itself on being a good neighbor within the city.
本校以能做市內的芳鄰感到欣慰。

注意：

to pride oneself on，與 to be proud of 或 to take pride in 意思都相似，只是用法和後面所跟的介詞不同而已。

· Mr. Lee takes great pride in becoming an American citizen.
李先生自傲成為美國公民。

· I am very proud of being a Chinese.
我以身為中國人為榮。

但如果說中國人因為 culture 和 heritage 的緣故，是個很自傲的民族，也可以說：The Chinese are a proud people.

proposition

◀) 078

 建議或主張

 例句

· Mr. A's proposition for our project was turned down.
A 先生對我們計畫的建議沒有被採納。

· I will consider his attractive proposition in this matter.
我會考慮他對這件事具有吸引力的主張。

動詞 要求結婚或為某事而提議（to propose for marriage or suggest for something）

例句

· The man regularly propositions his girlfriend for her hand in marriage.
這個人經常向他的女友求婚。（= He proposes marriage to her.）
（for her hand in marriage = ask her to marry him）

· The city council will proposition the state government for funds.
市議會將向州政府提出預算要求。

注意：

如果只說：" He propositions her." 通常是指要求做愛（sex）

或 She was propositioned by her boss.
她的老闆向她提出非分要求。（指 sex）

pump

◀)) 079

名詞 抽水機、打氣筒

例句

· Our water comes from the pump of a private well.
我們的水，是用抽水機從私人井裡抽出。

· I bought a bike with its pump.
我買了一部連打氣筒的自行車。

動詞 追問、探出

例句

· The police were trying to pump her about this murder case.
警察向她追問有關這起謀殺案件。

· He has pumped the full story out of his girlfriend.
他從女友處探出全盤事故。

· Pumping some information from the suspect could help solve
the problem.
追問嫌犯一些訊息有助解決問題。

radio

 080

名詞　收音機

· My wife usually listens to the radio every morning.
內人通常每天早上都聽收音機。

· The U.S. President sometimes speaks on nationwide radio.
美國總統有時在全國無線電廣播上談話。

動詞　廣播；通訊（to send a message）

例句

· At the airport, the lady radioed for a missing child.
在機場一位女士廣播尋找走失的孩子。

· All U.S. ships will have to radio the Coast Guard when they are in trouble.
所有美國船隻遇到困難時，應通知海岸巡邏隊。

· The doctor radioed the hospital to find out the status of his patient.
醫生電詢醫院以了解他病人的情況。

railroad

 081

名詞 鐵路

例句

- Some countries have more railroads than highways.
  有些國家鐵路比高速公路多。

- Railroad systems are not well developed in the small cities.
  在小城裡，鐵路系統發展欠佳。

動詞 不公正宣判或不公平待遇（但不用 railway）

例句

- The police tried to railroad this man to jail without further investigation.
  警察未經進一步調查，而把這位男士關進牢獄。

- With human rights, nobody should be railroaded.
  鑑於人權，不可待人不公平。

- Some Chinese feel that they have been railroaded by the court.
  有些中國人感到他們受到法院不公平的宣判。

- Mr. Wang thought his boss was railroading him.
  王先生覺得他老闆對他不公平。

reason

 082

 名詞 理由、原因

例句

· What was the reason for her tardiness?
她遲到的理由是什麼？

動詞 推理；說服（to think logically or to persuade）

例句

· Let's reason this matter all together.
讓我們一起認真商討這件事。（= think through）

· As she is a tough cookie, can you really reason with her?
她很固執，你真能說服她嗎？（tough cookie = very stubborn person）

· We have been reasoning with him for weeks.
我們勸他幾個禮拜了。

· I am reasoning that the break-in may be caused by someone in the neighborhood.
我推論盜竊可能是鄰近某人所造成。（= think out logically）

· He has reasoned with his boss for a pay raise.
他合情合理向老闆請求加薪。（= logically presented）

refuse

◀》 083

 拒絕 [rɪˋfjuz]

· I don't know why you always refuse to participate in our community services.
我不曉得你什麼老是拒絕參加社區服務。

 指「垃圾」[ˋrɛfjus]

· Don't put any refuse in my trash can.
不要在我的垃圾箱裡丟垃圾。
（refuse 當「垃圾」用時，通常單複數都一樣）

· The dump was so full that it had to refuse more refuse.
垃圾太滿了，所以拒收更多的垃圾。

right

◀》 084

 權利、正確或公正

· Everyone should have the right to a fair trial.
人人有權得到公正的審判。

· There is a difference between right and wrong.
有是非之別。（right 和 wrong 當抽象名詞，前面不加冠詞）

糾正或改正（多半指糾正法律或道德上的錯誤）

例句

- It's never too late to make an effort to right a wrong.
  糾正錯誤，不會嫌晚。

- Mr. A has righted the scandals in his office.
  A 先生的辦公室醜聞，已經改正過來。

 / 正確的、恰當的

例句

- Children should learn to say the right thing at the right time.
  孩子要學習在恰當的時間，說恰當的話。

- Many Americans don't know how to hold chopsticks right.
  許多美國人不知道怎樣拿好筷子。（right 當副詞，修飾動詞 hold）

sandwich

🔊 085

 三明治

例句

- Many people in the U.S. just eat a sandwich for lunch.
  在美國，許多人中餐只吃一個三明治。

 夾入或插入

例句

- The photo was sandwiched between two pages of the letter.
  照片夾在信中的兩頁。

- The receptionist will try to sandwich me between two appointments.
接待員想把我插入兩個約會中。

- I don't like being sandwiched in this conflict.
我不喜歡夾在雙方的糾紛中。

- The baby had been sandwiched between two big toys when I found him.
當我找到嬰孩時,他被夾在兩個大玩具之中。

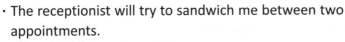

shot

◀)) 086

 打針;一杯酒;一張照片;彈頭;重要人物

例句

- The doctor gave him a shot.(醫生為他打針。)
(= injection,不過 shot 的後面不必說明打針的位置。所以不說: in the leg 或 in the arm。)

- He offered his girlfriend a shot at the bar.
他在酒吧裡請他女友喝杯酒。(= a small cup of liquor)

- That is a good shot of her.
她拍了一張好照片。(= a snap short = a picture)

- The physician took the gun shot out of his stomach.
醫生從他的胃部取出彈頭。(= bullet)

- He is a big shot.
他是大人物。(a big shot = VIP, very important person)

片語 a shot in the arm，意思是振奮人心或鼓舞士氣（boost of morale 或 encouragement）

 例句

· For administrative efficiency, computers are a shot in the arm.
對行政效率來說，電腦是令人鼓舞的。

· This gave him a shot in the arm.
這對他是個鼓勵。

形容詞 疲倦；機器壞了

例句

· The machine (motor) is (was) shot.
機器壞了。（shot = broken / out of order）
如果動詞用現在式 is 表示機器也許可以修理，但用過去式 was 則表示不能修理，已經作廢了。

· He exercises so much that he is shot.
他運動太多所以很累。（shot＝exhausted; tired）

 showcase

🔊 087

名詞 陳列櫃

例句

· Mr. B's dining room has a pretty showcase with different kinds of wine.
B 先生餐室的漂亮陳列櫃，排著各式各樣的酒。

· Jewelry stores always put diamond rings in their showcases.
首飾店都把鑽石戒指放在陳列櫃裡。

動詞 展覽或亮相（to highlight）

· The library is showcasing many rare items.
圖書館展出許多罕見的項目。

· The U.S. has showcased its military hardware such as tanks, missiles and artillery.
美國展示坦克、導彈、大砲等軍事裝備。

· The real estate company is showcasing many new houses in the newspaper.
房地產公司在報紙上展示許多新房子。

shy

◀)) 088

形容詞 害羞的；不足的、未達到

· Don't be too shy to tell your boyfriend what you think.
不必害羞；儘量告訴男友妳的想法。

· Some people are shyer of publicity than others.
有些人不愛拋頭露面。（shy 的形容詞比較級是：shyer, shyest 或 shier, shiest；也有人用 more shy, most shy）

· Mr. B died two months shy of his 100th birthday.
B 先生去世時，差兩個月 100 歲。

· John is one month shy of voting age.
John 離投票年齡還差一個月。

動詞 驚退、畏縮

例句

· The little girl shied in fright at the horrible movie scene.
小女孩看到可怕的電影鏡頭時，嚇得畏縮。

· Some people in the riot were shying stones at the police.
在暴動中，有些人向警察拋石頭。

· The horse was shying at the loud noise.
馬聽到大的聲音，就會害怕。

副詞 躲

例句

· Mr. A has fought shy of taking his stand on this issue.
A 先生閃躲不對這問題表示立場。（to fight shy of 閃躲）

soldier　　　🔊 089

名詞 士兵

例句

· Some young Chinese in the U.S. are willing to serve as American soldiers.
一些在美國年輕的中國人，願意擔任美國士兵。

· Mr. B is just a scholar; he is no soldier.
B 先生只是一位學者；他沒有作戰才能。

動詞 指不顧困難，堅持下去（to forge ahead no matter what difficulty is）

例句

· They are going to be soldiering on across a minefield.
他們不顧一切，勇往直前，通過佈雷地區。

· The Marine Corps usually have to soldier on under the hardest conditions.
陸戰隊通常在最艱難的情況下，仍要勇敢前進。

· He will soldier on whatever may happen.
不管發生什麼事，他仍要繼續幹下去。（通常 soldier 後面用 on）

spare

🔊 090

形容詞 多餘的、空閒的

例句

· Right now, he doesn't have any spare time as a translator.
現在他沒有多餘的時間擔任翻譯。

· Mr. A has two spare rooms for his relatives or friends.
A 先生有兩間多餘的房間供親友使用。

· Do you have any spare change?
你有多餘的零錢嗎？

動詞 免去或抽出

例句

· Could you spare a few minutes (to talk about the problem)?
你能抽出幾分鐘（談談這個問題）嗎？
（但不說：May I spare you for a few minutes?）

- I am sorry I have no time to spare at this moment.
  抱歉，此刻我抽不出時間來。（或 I really don't have the time to spare.）

- Don't spare the rod in school because you may spoil the child.
  在學校不能省掉鞭子，因為孩子會被寵壞。（就是學校要有處罰）

- The old man cannot spare a cane.
  老人家離不開手杖。

spoon

◀)) 091

名詞　湯匙
例句

- The patient had to be fed with a spoon.
  病人必須用湯匙餵著進食。

- Mr. A always puts two spoons of sugar in his coffee.
  A 先生在咖啡裡總是放兩匙的糖。

動詞　用匙取用；調情、求愛
例句

- At the table John spooned some syrup over / on the pancake.
  在餐桌上 John 用匙把糖漿澆在烘餅上。

- The young couple spoon all the time.
  一對年輕人，常在調情求愛。

- Mr. B was trying to spoon with her.
  B 先生與她做愛。

- I saw them spooning on the sofa when I entered the room.
  我走進房間時，看到他們在沙發上做愛。

stomach

 092

 胃、肚子

例句

· When you are hungry, your stomach sometimes starts to growl.
有時你餓時，肚子開始咕嚕咕嚕地叫。

 能吃；忍受

例句

· The patient was so sick that he couldn't even stomach liquids.
這位病人連流質也吃不下。（stomach = drink）

· She cannot stomach his poor manners.
她無法忍受他的粗魯。

· We have stomached many things we do not like.
我們對許多不喜歡的事，都得忍受。

· Many people are stomaching to deal with the complicated tax system.
許多人容忍複雜的納稅制度。

suit

093

 控告；全套衣服

例句

· My wife bought me a beautiful three-piece suit.
內人買給我一套漂亮的西裝。

three-piece suit 是指連帶男用背心的西裝，而 two-piece suit 是只有衣服和褲子的西裝。（suit 的複數是 suits）

· Mr. Yaung filed a suit against his old friend.
楊先生控告他的老朋友。（suit = law suit）

· Instead of paying her attorney for a law suit, she bought him an expensive suit.
她買了一套昂貴的服裝給她律師，以替代訴訟的費用。

動詞　合適

 例句

· Friday will suit me (fine).
星期五對我而言很適合。（suit = fit into my schedule）

但若用動詞 sue（控告），則後面不用 against：

· He will sue his boss for racial discrimination.
他控告老闆種族歧視。

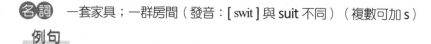

suite

🔊 094

名詞　一套家具；一群房間（發音：[swit] 與 suit 不同）（複數可加 s）

例句

· I like this bed-room suite very much.
我喜歡這套臥室家具。（suite = set）

· His office is located on the 4th floor, Suite 401.
他的辦公室是在四樓 401 室。

· The manager bought a living-room suite for his suite on the second floor.
經理為二樓辦公室買了一套客廳的家具。

sun

 095

 名詞　太陽；陽光

例句

· Many people say that China is the new rising sun in Asia.
許多人說，中國是亞洲新的太陽。

 動詞　曬太陽；使皮膚曬黑（to expose to the sun or to get tanned），後面多半跟反身代名詞 oneself（動詞時態是：sunned, sunning）

例句

· Some Americans like to sun themselves on / at the beach in summer.
夏天有些美國人喜歡在海灘上做日光浴。
（on the beach 多指在海灘上玩沙游水；at the beach 只是在海灘上。）

· The woman was sunning herself in her backyard.
這位女子在她後院曬太陽。

· Most Chinese women do not want to sun themselves.
多數中國女子不願曬太陽。

· The dog sunned itself in the front porch.
狗在前面陽台曬太陽。

註：sun 當動詞時，老外多半只指人或動物，很少指物品。所以「曬太陽」，不說「to sun the clothes」，只說：to hang the clothes out，或 to dry the clothes in the sun

table

◀)) 096

名詞　桌子

例句

- We reserved a table for ten at a restaurant.
  我們在餐館預定了十個座位的桌子。

- I always keep some books on my bedside table.
  我常在床邊的桌上放幾本書。

動詞　開會時延期討論提案等，也就是暫緩審議（to postpone discussion of a bill or suggestion until future time）

例句

- They tabled the motion at the meeting.
  他們在會議中延緩討論提案。
  （motion 就是 suggestion 或 idea）

- I made the motion and he seconded it.
  我提案，他同意。
  （second 的意思是贊成；to second the motion 也就是附議）

- After I seconded the motion at the meeting, he tabled it.
  在我附議後，他延後討論了。

- We are tabling this matter until further notice.
  我們延期討論這件事，以後再說。

- The issue has been tabled for months, but our position has not been changed.
  這個問題延期討論幾個月了，但我們立場仍然不變。

take

🔊 097

 取得；帶往；花費

· Mr. A took the first place in the speech contest.
A 先生演講比賽第一名。

· Will this bus take me to the railway station?
這路公車能帶我到火車站嗎？

· It has taken two hours for me to write this long letter.
寫這封長信，花我兩小時。

名詞 立場、反應或收入額

例句

· The mayor and city council will discuss their take on gambling policy.（= standpoint）
市長和市議會將討論他們對賭博政策的立場。

· What is your doctor's take on your symptoms ?
醫生對你的症狀看法如何？（= view）

· The government's spending has outstripped its take.
政府的開支超過收入。（= income）

taxing

◀)) 098

名詞 tax：稅

例句

- Uncle Sam is trying to tax its citizens very heavily.
  美國政府對其人民課以重稅。
  （山姆叔叔：「Uncle Sam」= American government）

動詞 tax：徵稅；影響（harm）

例句

- To use too much chicken waste may tax the water system.
  使用太多的雞糞也許會影響到飲水系統

形容詞 taxing：累人的；費勁的；困難的；繁重的（tiring, troublesome, difficult or demanding）

例句

- Writing a dissertation can be very taxing.
  寫篇論文是很累人的。

- It may seem taxing for her to deal with people because of her sheltered background.
  由於她的受寵背景，與人相處似乎有點困難。
  （sheltered = protective）

- The IRS is trying to make tax systems more taxing.
  稅務局把納稅制度變得更繁瑣。
  （IRS = Internal Revenue Service）

tear

🔊 099

 撕破 [tɛr] ；眼淚 [tir]（發音不同）

例句

- Could a tear be used as a symbol of love?
  眼淚可以做為愛的象徵嗎？

- He found a big tear in his car seat.
  他在汽車座位上發現一大破洞。

- Upon seeing the tear in the famous painting, she shed a tear.
  看到名畫被撕破後，她流出眼淚。（動詞 shed 的過去式及過去分詞也是 shed）（第一個 tear 是撕破；第二個是眼淚）

 撕破 [tɛr]

例句

- His words are tearing my heart apart.
  他的言語撕裂了我的心。

telling

🔊 100

 tell：告訴

例句

- He was telling me what happened in the past weeks.
  他告訴我過去幾個星期所發生的事情。（進行式）

- Telling the truth is the best policy in one's life.
  說實話是一個人生活的最上策。（動名詞）

形容詞 telling：有效的；有力的，或表示對某種事情正面或負面的
一種心裡反映或流露（revealing or image reflecting）

例句

· The way she dresses is very telling.
她的穿著，顯露她內心的感受。

· At the meeting, he made a telling remark.
開會時，他做了一次有效的評論。

· Whenever he talks to me, he has a telling smile.
他每次與我說話總是帶著一種流露內心感情的微笑。

· That many Americans call the best students nerds is very telling.
許多美國人稱呼好學生為「nerd」，給人負面的感受。

（nerd 是指那些只會讀書考試，而不善於為人處事，與社會現實幾乎
脫節的「書呆子」）

 tip   ◁)) 101

名詞 忠告；小費

例句

· Speaking of stocks, I will take your tip.
談到股票方面，我倒要接受你的忠告。

· The waiter gave me a good tip and I left him a large tip.
侍者給我一個好忠告，我也給他較多的小費。（tip = advice）

通知（to tip off = to inform）

· She will tip off the police about an illegal operation.
她要通知警察一個違法的勾當。

top

◄)) 102

 頂端

例句

· Mr. A has risen to the top of his career.
A 先生的事業達到頂峰。

· There is a temple on the top of the hill.
山頂上有間寺廟。

 做得更好，或高過某人（to do something better or to be taller than someone）

例句

· If he had tried harder, he could have topped his class.
假如他以前用功他就會名列前茅。

· He thinks he can top it.
他想他會做得最好。（it 代表 anything）

· The tax-cut issue will top today's agenda.
減稅問題將是今天主要議題。

· Mr. Lin tops me by three inches.
林先生比我高出三吋。

treasure

🔊 103

 寶物或財富

例句

· Your trash could be someone's treasure.
你的垃圾，也許是別人的寶貝。

 珍惜或珍愛（to hold dear or to value）（動詞時態是：treasured, treasuring）

例句

· We will treasure these moments with our dear friends.
我們珍惜與好友相聚的時刻。（treasure = cherish）

· I always treasure the friendship with good people.
我一向珍愛好人的友誼。

· My wife and I have treasured very much our children's wedding albums.
內人和我都很珍惜兒女的結婚相簿。

unashamedly

🔊 104

 ashamed 是「羞恥的」；unashamed 就是「不羞恥的」

例句

· He feels ashamed for what he has done to his friends.
他對朋友的所作所為感到慚愧。

· The child seems unashamed about his poor grades.
這孩子功課差，而不害臊。

副詞 unashamedly 不是「不羞恥」，而是「公開地」（openly），「明顯地」（obviously）

例句

· This information is unashamedly based on his careful research.
這資料很明顯的是根據他細心的研究。

· I am unashamedly proud of being a Chinese.
我很公開的表示以身為中國人為榮。

unqualifiedly

 動詞 qualify：合格、勝任；unqualify：不合格

例句

· I feel he qualifies for this post.
我覺得他勝任這份工作。（post = position）

名詞 qualification：合格；勝任（但沒有名詞 unqualification）

例句

· The interviewee seems to meet all the qualifications.
這位應試者似乎符合所有的資格。

 qualified 夠資格的；unqualified：不夠資格的、不適合的

例句

· He is an unqualified engineer.
他是位不夠資格的工程師。

 105

Part 1
art 2
art 3
art 4
art 5

副詞 unqualifiedly：不是不夠資格，反而是「非常夠資格」、「絕對勝任」（extremely qualified）（多半用在推薦方面）（unqualifiedly = very qualified）

例句

· I can recommend Miss Su unqualifiedly for this high position.
我推薦非常夠資格的蘇小姐擔任這份高職。

· His credentials are unqualifiedly perfect for the job.
他的證件資歷是完全可以勝任這份工作。

welcome ◀》 106

動詞 歡迎

例句

· Welcome (you) to my home.
歡迎光臨寒舍。

· I will welcome you with open arms.
我將熱誠地歡迎你。

有時後面跟著其他的片語或表示歡迎的某種動作

例句

· Mr. Clinton was welcomed with respectful applause.
克林頓先生受到恭敬的歡迎掌聲。

· You are welcomed every time you come.
你每次來都受到歡迎。

· Mr. Lee is being welcomed.
李先生正在接受歡迎。

 歡迎的

- You are welcome.
  不客氣。

- Parents are welcome to our school.
  歡迎父母到我們學校來。

名詞

例句

- Thank you for your warm welcome.
  謝謝你熱烈的歡迎。

- He wears out their welcome.
  他自己破壞了人家的歡迎。

- I wore out my welcome.
  我破壞了人家的歡迎。（動詞時態：wear, wore worn）

- You have worn out your welcome.
  你破壞了別人對你的歡迎。

※ 這裡的 wear out 是指人家對你的歡迎，卻被你自己的不自愛或不為主人著想等原因而破壞了（spoil）。諸如做客不能久住，否則就會被主人討厭。難怪 Ben Franklin 說過：Fish and guests sting after three days.（魚和客人一樣，三天後就會變臭）。

wound

 107

名詞　傷口 [wund]

例句

・The nurse used the bandage to wind up the wound.
護士用繃帶紮緊傷口。

動詞　wind [waɪnd]：wind 的過去式及過去分詞也是 wound [waʊnd]，意思是「纏繞」。

例句

・The bandage was wound around the wound.
繃帶纏繞著傷口。

- -

名詞　wind [wɪnd]：風

例句

・The wind blew off my hat.
風吹走了我的帽子。

- -

動詞　wind：繃緊 [waɪnd]

例句

・I need to wind the old clock every morning.
每天早晨我要為老鐘上發條。

・The wind was too strong to wind the sail.
風太大，所以紮不緊船帆。

wrong

 壞事；邪惡

例句

- Everyone should know right from wrong.
  每個人要能辨別是非。

- Since he became a high-ranking official, Mr. A has committed many wrongs.（wrongs = crimes）
  自從 A 先生當了高官後，他犯下許多罪行。

 冤枉；虐待；委屈

例句

- Many innocent Chinese were wronged by being sentenced to capital punishment.
  許多無辜的中國人，冤枉被判死刑。

- I can't tolerate her wronging his young stepson.
  她對他繼子的虐待，我無法容忍。

 錯誤的、壞的

例句

- Many Americans have been given some wrong information about the Chinese people.
  許多美國人被告知一些對中國人不實的信息。

- It is very wrong of him to mislead a young girl in such a way.
  他如此把一位少女引入歧途，是居心不良。

副詞 不好

_例句_

· Some Chinese people are treating their fellow countrymen all wrong.
有些中國人，對待自己同胞太差了。（wrong 是副詞，修飾動詞 are treating）

Part 2　流行的字詞

　　語言與文字，有時也跟著社會而演變。英語裡也有許多「流行」的單字，其中也包括一些拉丁文或法文，甚至有人「創造」了一些新字。以下介紹的單字都是平時生活中常用、常見的單字。

Part 2　流行的字詞

acrimonious

🔊 109

 意思是刻薄，厲害或苛烈（bitter or harsh in temper or manner）（其名詞是 acrimony）

例句

- The couple have tried to make the divorce less acrimonious.
  這對夫婦儘量減少離婚的刻薄程度。

- The talks between the two countries seemed more acrimonious than before.
  兩國間的會談似乎比過去更苛烈。

- Mr. A's acrimony in his opinion may cause some unpleasant consequences.
  A 先生對他自己意見的刻薄，也許造成不好的後果。

ad hoc

🔊 110

這是拉丁文，指特別的，專門的，或有特殊的委員會或開會（a particular committee or meeting）

例句

- As the ad hoc committee chairperson, he announced a new additional member.
  他以特別委員會主席身份，宣佈一名新增委員。

· The college president created an ad hoc advisory group to assist him in decision-making.
大學校長設立一個特別顧問小組，協助他政策性的決定。

bittersweet

 ◄)) 111

 意思是苦中有甜，甜中有苦（both bitter and sweet; pleasant and sad）

例句

· Falling in love can be a kind of bittersweet experience.
談戀愛是一種有苦有甜的經驗。

· Graduations and weddings are considered as bittersweet times.
畢業和婚禮，也被認為有苦有甜的時刻。

· After five years of bittersweet romance, the couple broke up.
經過五年的甜苦戀愛，這對情侶分手了。

consensus

◄)) 112

 意思是多數人的意見，或意見一致。
（general agreement in opinion; an opinion held by all or most）

例句

· The consensus is to postpone our new project until next year.
多數人的意見，是要把我們的計畫延到明年。

- We are glad that we have reached a consensus with the other party.
  我們與其他一派意見一致，感到高興。

但動詞 consent 是同意或贊同：
- Chinese people will never consent to another civil war.
  中國人絕不同意再有內戰。

constituency

◀》 113

- -

 指選區的一群選民或一批擁護者（group of voters or supporters）（複數是 constituencies）

例句

- This scholar candidate has a wide constituency in the education field.
  這位學者出身的候選人，擁有一批廣大教育界的選民。

- His constituencies are composed of people from all walks of life.
  擁護他的群眾，包括各個行業的人民。

- Some politicians change the ways they deal with different constituencies.
  一些政客改變他們處理不同選區支持者的方式。

但名詞 constituent 係指個別的選民（individual voter）

例句

- Constituents do not always remain faithful to a candidate.
  選民對一位候選人，未必能忠心耿耿。

devastate

 114

 破壞、垮掉、身心交瘁（to destroy; to feel helpless or empty）（形容詞是 devastating；名詞是 devastation）

例句

· The parents are devastated by their son's financial difficulty.
父母對兒子的財務困難極感無奈。

· To Mr. B, your criticism can be quite devastating.
你對 B 先生的批評，令他十分洩氣。

· The majority of Chinese people are still feeling the devastation over (the) Japanese invasion in WW II.
多半中國人仍然感受到二次世界大戰日本侵略的破壞。

dilemma

 115

 進退兩難的窘境或困境（to be caught in a difficult situation）

例句

· China's dilemma is that it has required Taiwan to accept the "one China" policy as a pre-condition for opening direct "three links" with China.
中國的困境是要台灣接受「一中」作為直接「三通」的前提。

103

簡單地說，就是：

· China has been in a dilemma over the Taiwan issue.
  中國對台灣問題感到進退兩難。

· The teacher is in a dilemma over his students' disciplinary problems.
  老師對他學生的懲罰問題感到十分困擾。

· The dilemma I am facing is if I have to tell him the truth.
  我面臨的窘境就是能否告訴他真相。

· If this problem occurs, we may be in a dilemma.
  假如這個問題發生，我們也陷入兩難。

ecstatic

🔊 116

形容詞 狂喜的，心醉心迷的（great delight; being overpowered by joy）（名詞是 ecstasy，但形容詞 ecstatic 較常用）

 例句

· Mr. A was ecstatic at receiving his girlfriend's letter.
  A 先生收到女友信件時，非常高興。

· If your son can find a job and support himself, you will be ecstatic.
  假如你兒子能找到工作而自立更生，你將會十分開心。

· Many Chinese people were in ecstasy over the result of Taiwan's election.
  許多老中對台灣的選舉結果極感滿意。
  （如用 in ecstasy 則為「華麗」字眼）

El Nino

◀)) 117

西班牙文，與 greenhouse effects 的意思相似，都是指全球變溫問題
（global warming）

例句

· Many people around the world are concerned about El Nino.
世人都在關心全球變溫問題。（有人譯為「埃爾尼諾」）

· El Nino has made our weather unpredictable.
「埃爾尼諾」現象使我們的氣候難以預料。

entourage

◀)) 118

 這是法文，指隨行人員（a group of associates），發音
（antoorazh）

例句

· Our university president and an entourage of 20 scholars
visited China last week.
我們大學校長與廿名隨行的學者，上週訪問中國。

· The movie star and his entourage disturbed everyone in the
restaurant.
這位明星和他的隨員擾亂了餐館每個人。

· The premier's 30-member entourage will have meetings with
their counter partners.
總理的卅位隨行人員，將與對方搭檔舉行會談。

episode

 119

名詞 意思是一些令人可笑或不好的插曲,或一生中的一段經驗
(single event of something)

例句

· My friend had an episode with his asthma.
我朋友的氣喘給他一些人生不好的插曲。

· His divorce was an unpleasant episode in his life.
他的離婚是他人生中一段意外的經驗。

· The TV news reporter had a laughing episode in front of camera.
電視新聞主播在攝影機前出了一段令人可笑的插曲。(可能讀錯了字或犯某些錯誤)

· While giving his speech, Mr. A had an episode of laughing.
A 先生演講時,有個可笑的小插曲。(為自己犯了小毛病而自嘲等)

esprit de corps

 120

名詞 法文,指團隊精神,士氣高昂,熱心為大眾的榮譽而努力。
(common spirit, or inspiring enthusiasm and strong regards for the group honor)(多半當名詞用)

例句

· Chinese people should develop an esprit de corps in all fields.
中國人應該在各個領域裡提高團隊合作精神。

- We need to cultivate esprit de corps in our children.
我們應該薰陶孩子的團隊合作精神。

faux pas

◀) 121

法文，（發音 fopa），係指一種錯誤或有失檢點（an error or mistake）

- He finally committed his faux pas yesterday.
昨天他終於承認錯誤。

- I behave carefully because I don't want to commit a faux pas.
我行為謹慎，唯恐有失檢點。（動詞多半用 commit）

fiasco

◀) 122

名詞　意思是一連串不愉快的事情，也可能是完全的失敗或可笑可恥的結局（a series of unpleasant events）

例句

- This party turned out to be a fiasco.
這場派對發生了不愉快的事情。

- The new play at the theater was a fiasco.
戲院所演的新戲徹底失敗了。

- After divorce his child's visitation has turned into a fiasco.
離婚後他對孩子的探視權產生一連串的問題。

· We will try to avoid a fiasco by planning carefully.
我們要小心計畫，以免產生不愉快的結果。

雖然 fiasco 通常只用單數，但有時也有人用複數。
· I know of several fiascos in her life.（或 fiascoes）

foolproof ◀) 123

這個名詞係從「防水」、「防火」（waterproof, fireproof）等字模仿而來，人們又增加了childproof, baby proof 等字，意思是：「預防……使不致……」（to protect something from going wrong）

例句

· All the toys in the market should be baby proof and childproof.
市場上的所有玩具，必須使嬰兒和孩童有安全的保障。

· The salesperson told me that the lawn mower was foolproof.
店員告訴我鋤草機的品質優良不易損壞。
（也就是鋤草機有預防損壞的設計，使你不致吃虧受騙，成為傻瓜）

froufrou ◀) 124

法文，名詞：意思是過份的華麗裝飾或矯揉造作的雅致（overly decorated or something too fancy）

例句

· At the party we felt that her dress was a little froufrou.
在宴會中，我們覺得她的穿著有點過份華麗。

- The building contains too much froufrou.
這個建築物包括太多的華麗裝飾。

- The froufrou of this new library seems to be incredible.
這個新圖書館的過份裝飾令人難以置信。

- Her life seems nothing but froufrou.
她的生活只是矯揉造作而已。

但也有人把 froufrou 當做奢侈的意思（luxurious）

 例句

- This Rolex watch is too froufrou for me.
這個勞力士錶對我來說太奢侈了。

- The spending habit of his froufrou seems immature.
他的奢侈習慣顯得不成熟。

gridlock

◀)) 125

名詞 指交通堵塞或停滯（to be stuck）

例句

- The U.S. government is concerned with the partisan gridlock on the health care issue.
美國政府擔心黨派行為對健保議題造成停滯。

- Many cities in China were mired in traffic gridlock during the Lunar New Year.
許多中國城市在春節期間陷入交通大堵塞。

· Do you think freedom and democracy may sometimes create gridlock in the normal political process?
你認為自由和民主，有時會造成正常政局操作的停滯嗎？

henpeck

🔊 126

動詞 指老公受到老婆的控制，或常受老婆嘮嘮叨叨責罵不休，也就是懼內，怕老婆或「妻管嚴」（completely dominated by one's wife）（照字義 hen 是母雞，peck 是啄，也就是會啄的母雞。）

例句

· The timid man was constantly henpecked by his wife.
膽小兮兮的男子，常被老婆管得死死的。

· Has Dr. Lin been henpecked all the time?
林博士常常怕他的太座嗎？

· Wives are not supposed to henpeck their spouses.
太座不應該對自己「另一半」管得太嚴。
但是怕老公的老婆，一般不說：She is henpecked. (×) 即使老公很嚴，也沒有「會啄的公雞」（rooster-peck）的說法。

homeschooling

當名詞或動名詞，指一些美國人認為公立學校水平差，不願把兒女送到學校，寧可留在家裡教育（Parents keep their children at home for education.）（多半由父母擔任教師）

例句

· Homeschooling has become one of the optional education programs.
孩子在家受教育，已成為選擇性的教育項目之一。

· Home schoolers have brought more responsibilities to the librarians.
在家受教育的孩子帶給圖書館的專業人員更多的責任。
（home school 後面加 er，變成在家受教育的孩子）也可當動詞使用。

例句

· Many children are home schooled in the U.S.
在美國許多孩子在家受教育。

hysterical

🔊 128

 指情緒異常激動，難以控制（emotionally uncontrolled）（有人說成歇斯底里）

例句

· The woman got hysterical and started crying.
這位女子情緒非常激動，大哭起來。

· How to end things with his hysterical girlfriend has become his problem.
如何與他那位情緒異常的女友分手，成了他的問題。

但是 hysterics 這個名詞，是指狂野情緒爆發症。而名詞 hysteric 是指這種病的患者。

例句

· Mr. B started seeing a physician because of his hysterics.
B 先生因為患有狂野情緒爆發症而看醫生。

· The doctor diagnosed Mr. B as a hysteric.
醫生診斷 B 先生是位狂野情緒爆發者。

infrastructure

◀)) 129

名詞 指一個國家人民賴以生存的基本結構或基礎建設，諸如通訊、教育、運輸、動力等等，也就是 internal structure。雖然也可以說成 foundation or basis of something，但這比 foundation 的意義較為廣泛。

例句

· China's infrastructure should catch up with its economic development.
中國的國家基礎建設必須要趕上它的經濟發展。

或簡單地說：

· China needs to develop its infrastructure.
中國必須發展基本的國家建設。

- Taiwan has lifted the ban on infrastructure and advance technology to China.
台灣對中國大陸的基本建設和高科技的轉移已經解禁。

- The infrastructure of the city consists of many elements.
都市的基本結構包括許多要素。

- Mr. A designed the infrastructure of auto factories.
A 先生設計了汽車工廠的基本結構。

至於 foundation 又是指一般性的基礎

- Hardwork can be a foundation of success.
努力工作是成功的基礎。

- Education is a foundation for (cultivating) responsible citizens.
教育是培養認真負責國民的基礎。

insinuate

◀)) 130

動詞 意思是暗示，旁敲側擊，或含沙射影（to hint or imply indirectly）（名詞是 insinuation）

例句

- Mrs. A insinuates that they will not finish up their project by next month.
A 太太暗示他們在下月前不能完成他們的計畫。

- Over the past months, Bob has insinuated that the couple will get a divorce.
過去幾個月來，Bob 暗示這對夫婦會離婚。

· Your insinuation on this problem really upsets me.
你對這個問題的旁敲側擊，實在令我不爽。

jeopardize (=jeopardise)

 131

 意思是危及或損害，也就是處於危險境地或冒著危險去做某事。（to cause some danger or to make the situation worse）

例句

· Mr. Chen's outspokenness may jeopardize his position at the university.
陳先生的直言不諱，也許對他在大學工作造成不利。

· We should not sue our boss because we do not want to jeopardize our working environment.
我們不可控告老闆，因為我們不要損害工作的環境。

名詞 jeopardy

例句

· If the airlines do not have a sound maintenance policy, all passengers' lives will be in jeopardy.
航空公司如果沒有良好的修護制度，就會危及旅客的生命安全。
（airline 是航空公司；airliner 是指飛機）

· Many police put their lives in jeopardy every day.
許多警察每天的生命都在危險中。

knockout

 名詞 意思是異常動人或漂亮,可指人或物(someone or something beautiful or great)

例句

· Her red dress is really a knockout.
她穿的紅色衣服真是漂亮迷人。

· His new girlfriend is a knockout.
他的新女友,美得令人傾倒。

也有擊倒,擊昏或傑作的意思。

例句

· The boxer gave his opponent a knockout punch.
拳擊者給他對手重重的一擊。(knockout = real hard)

· Do you think Mr. Clinton's memoir will be a knockout?
你想柯林頓的回憶錄是部傑作嗎?

動詞

· He was knockedout by a mighty blow.
他被重擊擊昏。
(mighty blow = heavy punch)

· Mr. A knockedout his opponent in the ring.
A 先生在拳擊場中將對手擊倒。
(**注意**:動詞的過去式和過去分詞是 knockedout,而不是 knockouted)

也有人把 knock out 分開使用：
· When she insulted him, he knocked her out.
　當她侮辱他，他把她打倒。

la-la land

🔊 133

意思是異想天開，不切實際（unrealistic; not in real world）據說這個字是從洛杉磯（L.A.）而來，因為 L.A. 是好萊塢的美國電影業中心，有人誤認為是世外桃源。

例句

· I think Mr. A is in la-la land.
　我想 A 先生在異想天開。（當名詞）

· Many young people have la-la land habits.
　許多年青人有不切實際的習慣。（當形容詞）

landslide

🔊 134

 一般是指競選時得到壓倒性的勝利，也就是得到絕大多數的選票而勝利（overwhelming victory mostly in election or in other competition）

例句

· Mr. Clinton won a landslide victory over Mr. Dole in 1996.
　柯林頓先生在 1996 年與杜爾先生競選時，得到壓倒性的勝利。

· He won an unexpected landslide victory for re-election.

也可以指競選的慘敗：
- Mr. A lost the election by a landslide.
  A 先生選舉慘敗。

但是如果照字面意義，又是指滑坡崩塌：

例句

- Many houses were destroyed in the landslide after the heavy rains.
  許多房子因豪雨而崩塌。

macho

🔊 135

西班牙文，指男性的雄壯活力（aggressive or exhibits masculine）
（當形容詞）

例句

- He always wears a short-sleeve shirt in chilly days; he must be macho.（= a macho man）
  他常在冷天裡穿短袖襯衫；他一定是位健壯的男人。

- Bill made a macho move in order to impress the girl.
  Bill 的一副男子強壯動作，為要取得女孩欽佩。

但指女子強悍剛勇時，則用 amazon：
- She always likes to act as an amazon type.
  她常常喜歡裝著有男子氣剛強的女子。

mainstreaming

🔊 136

名詞 多半指安排殘障兒童轉入正規學習環境（bring physically handicapped children into regular classrooms）

例句

· Over the past years mainstreaming has been a kind of American educational policy.
過去多年來，把殘障學童轉入正規學習環境，已成為美國教育政策之一。

· Actually, some educators do not want to accept the idea of mainstreaming.
其實一些教育者不接受這種安排殘障兒童轉入正規班級的主張。

動詞 mainstream：也就是把殘障兒童轉入正規班級

例句

· Physically challenged students are being mainstreamed into the regular classes.
身體殘障學生正在轉入正規的教室上課。（physically challenged 比 physically handicapped 較為婉轉、禮貌）

· How to mainstream in Chinese schools can be advocated at the meeting.
如何在中國學校把殘障學生轉入正規學習環境，可在會議中加以提倡。

mea culpa

🔊 137

這是拉丁文,意思是「我的錯」(my fault)

老外為了表現文明禮貌,所以當別人道歉時,自己也說:「不是你的錯,而是我的錯」(Pardon me, mea culpa!)

例句

· I am sorry, mea culpa! = It is my fault. = I am at fault.
(或且只說 mea culpa 也可以)

· With his mea culpa personality, Mr. A is well liked by his associates.
A 先生個性謙卑,受到同仁喜愛。

mechanism

🔊 138

 名詞 本來意思是機械裝置或機關結構,但一般美國人也把它用在解決問題的實際辦法或途徑(specific procedures or practical ways to resolve something)

例句

· They focused on a mechanism to resolve difficult issues rather than disagreeing over them.
他們集中精力於解決問題的方法,而不是只對問題的反對。

· Mechanisms are in use to combat tax evasion.
實際的方法使用在打擊逃稅上。

· Teachers will use a specific mechanism to teach their students.
老師使用特殊的方法教導他們的學生。

- It seems that we have no mechanism for changing his decision.
我們似乎沒有辦法能改變他的決定。

- Has China set up a mechanism to control its national economy?
中國已設立了一個能控制國家經濟的機構嗎？

moocher

🔊 139

這個名詞係指常常佔人家便宜，或喜歡揩油的人（a person always takes advantage of others）

此外，還有 sponger 或 freeloader 意義很相近。不過，這兩個字，多指吃飯或住宿等方面的揩油，而 moocher 的範圍較廣。

例句

- Some friends consider Mr. Smith a moocher.
一些朋友認為 Smith 先生是位喜歡佔人便宜的人

- Try not to borrow things (too) frequently from your neighbors or friends, or they may think you are a moocher, sponger or freeloader.
儘量不要常常向鄰居或朋友借東西，以免他們認為你是一位揩油者。

outsourcing

◀》 140

 **名詞** / **動名詞**

意思是外部採辦或外購，也就是原來自己內部的事是自行經辦，後改向外面聘請專業人員處理，以減少費用。（hiring people or receiving services from outside companies; not in-house services）

例句

· Currently, outsourcing has become a popular trend within organizations.
目前聘請外面人員處理內部事務變成各機關流行的趨向。

· It is said that outsourcing is helping (to) save money in the long run.
據說外發採辦，最終還能省錢。

動詞 outsource

例句

· Over the past years our school outsourced a significant part of the campus bookstore operations.
過去幾年中，我們學校的書店大部份作業是聘雇外面人員經營。

outweigh

🔊 141

名詞 意思是超過，比……重要（more important or more valuable）（通常當動詞）

例句

· You can see that the advantage far outweighs the disadvantage.
你能看到優點遠超過缺點。

· Mr. A's merits may have outweighed his past mistakes.
A 先生的功勞已超過他過去的錯誤。

· Our happiness should outweigh our desire for material things.
我們的幸福應該比物質慾望重要。

overwhelming

🔊 142

形容詞 意思是勢不可擋；壓倒的（with great force or deep emotion）

例句

· For Mr. B, his girlfriend's (sexy) temptations seem overwhelming.
對 B 先生而言，他女友的性感誘惑，似乎難以抵制。

· Mr. Ma was elected by an overwhelming majority of votes.
馬先生得到壓倒性的選票而當選。

動詞 overwhelm：壓倒或極度

例句

· The candidate took over 55% of the ballots and overwhelmed his opponent.
候選人取得百分五十五的投票結果而壓倒他的對手。

· When Mr. Wang met his girlfriend, he was overwhelmed with joy.
當王先生看到他的女友，他極度興奮。

paparazzo

◀》143

義大利文，指專門跟隨名人報導他們私生活的攝影記者（a photographer who takes pictures of private lives of the well-known figures）（當名詞）

例句

· Mr. B has long been known as a paparazzo.
眾人皆知，B 先生是跟蹤名人、報導他們私生活的攝影記者。（狗仔隊）

· Some celebrities have been annoyed by paparazzi.（複數）
一些名人受到跟隨的攝影記者，感到厭煩。

parameter

◀》144

 意思是某些事情的界限或限制（limit to something）

例句

· I will promote him within the parameter(s) of my authority.
我要在我有限的權力內提拔他。

· Many people can only donate to charity based on the parameter of their fixed income.
許多人對慈善的樂捐只能限在固定的收入內。

· I will try my best to make some contributions to this university within the parameter(s) of my ability.
我願在我的能力範圍內為本校做出貢獻。

paranoid

🔊 145

形容詞 多疑的，有妄想多疑傾向（to be oversuspicious）

例句

· I don't know why Mr. B is getting so paranoid today.
我不曉得 B 先生今天為什麼這樣疑神疑鬼。

名詞 指多疑症患者

例句

· Being such a paranoid, Mr. A always argues with his wife.
A 先生是位多疑症患者，他常與他妻子爭吵。

但 paranoia 是名詞，指一種精神病症：
· Work difficulties and paranoia may walk hand in hand.
工作上的困難和妄想多疑症，也許有密切關係。

per se

◀)) 146

拉丁文，意思是事情的本身（in itself; as such）是一種加強語氣（當形容詞）

 例句

· Many people know very little about library operations per se.
許多人對圖書館本身的作業，知道得很少。

· Money per se will not create a problem if it is well-managed.
金錢本身不會造成問題假如處理得好。（it 指金錢）

poohbah

◀)) 147

名詞 指那些身兼數職或自命不凡的要人，也指能力不夠，工作不能勝任的主管或高官（incompetent persons with high positions）

例句

· We did not want a bunch of poohbahs telling us how to run our business.
我們不要那些工作不能勝任的高官告訴我們如何經營事業。

· Our school will not hire a new poohbah right away for this important job.
我們學校不會馬上聘請一位不能稱職的人擔任這個重要的工作。

· In most cases poohbahs are not well-respected.
一般而言，身兼數職不能勝任的高官，是不受尊敬的。

prerogative

🔊 148

 但這個字看來像是形容詞。意思是獨有的權利（exclusive privilege or right）

例句

· If you don't want to be around, that is your prerogative.
假如你不要在這裡，那是你自己的權利。

· Voting has become the prerogative of all adult citizens.
選舉已成為成年國民特有的權利。

· To be an ambassador is not just a male prerogative.
擔任大使職務，不僅僅是男子獨有的權利。

presumptuous

🔊 149

 意思是放肆的、冒昧的（show over-confidence; too bold or forward）

例句

· Mr. B's remarks about our boss would seem to be presumptuous to me.
B 先生對我們老闆的評論，我認為似乎很放肆。

· It is presumptuous for anyone to attend a party without an invitation.
任何人未經邀請而參加宴會，是很冒昧。

名詞 presumption 又有自作推測的意思

· You presumption that I will be able to get a part-time job is not true.
你的推測我會找個半職工作，是不確實的。

pro bono

 🔊 150

拉丁文，意思是為社會提供免費服務（free service for the good of society）（多半當形容詞）

例句

· The lawyer rendered the service pro bono for the needy.
律師為窮人提供免費服務。

· It would be wonderful if more physicians could help the old and the poor pro bono!
假如更多醫師能為老人和窮人免費服務，那該多好！
（形容詞前加冠詞 the，係指一般性，如：the rich, the poor, the needy 等）

repatriate

🔊 151

 動詞 意思是遣返回國（send back to the country of birth）（名詞是 repatriation）

例句

· The murderer will be repatriated to his homeland after the investigations are completed.
調查完畢後，謀殺兇手將被遣返回國。

· The prisoners of war are generally repatriated to their countries.
戰犯通常是要遣送回到他們的國家。

· Repatriation has been requested by the Chinese government for its corrupt officials overseas.
中國政府要求把海外的貪汙官員遣送回國。

註：動詞 deport 是指依照法律把外國人驅逐出境，也是 repatriation 的一種方式。其名詞是 deportation。

savory

🔊 152

（= savoury）這是形容詞，多半是指美味可口的食品（very tasty of food or delicious）

例句

· This turkey meat is very savory.
這火雞肉的味道很好。

· I consider this dish to be savory.
我認為這盤菜很好吃。

有時也指令人愉快可喜的事：
· I have read a savory article from the newspaper.
我從報紙上看到一篇有味的文章。

然而，常用的 unsavory，又是指一個人在行為或性格上有種令人不悅的古怪。

例句

· He appeared to be rather unsavory.
他看起來有點怪怪的。

· 或 He seemed to be an unsavory character (person).
他好像是位壞傢伙。

savvy

 🔊 153

形容詞 意思是聰明，機智，有豐富的知識（intelligent and knowledgeable）

例句

· Professor Thrash has been savvy about the English language.
Thrash 教授對英語的知識非常豐富。

· Mary is a successful and savvy woman in her business career.
Mary 在事業上是位成功而機智的女士。

· Being energetic and savvy, Mr. A has become popular in our campus.
精力充沛而聰明的 A 先生，在我們校園裡廣受歡迎。
（**注意**：不要與另一個形容詞 savory 弄錯）

scenario

🔊 154

名詞 影劇上的特有名稱，來自義大利文，原意是描寫影劇的情節或提綱，其結局如何，往往要等到最後才能知道。所以被人以「借喻法」引用為預料將來一種或好或壞，或簡單或複雜的局面。（any situation in the future, good or bad, simple or complicated; possible future events; something may lead to a possible situation）

例句

· The tension between China and Taiwan makes for a bad scenario.
中國與台灣的緊張情勢，將來可能造成不良的局面。

· If the U.S. does not handle the Taiwan issue carefully, who knows what scenario could happen？
假如美國不謹慎處理台灣問題，誰知道將來又會發生什麼結局呢？

· In my opinion, to be a single parent is not a good scenario.
我認為單親不是一個很好的局面。

· When the parents get a divorce, it may not be a good scenario for the children.
父母離婚，對孩子可能是不好的局面。

· Throughout the entire scenario, he proved to be extremely helpful.
在整個過程中，他證明是位非常得力的助手。

showdown

 155

名詞 意思是最後的攤牌或關鍵時刻，也有反對摩擦的味道（final confrontation or critical moment or disagreement）

例句

· I think there always be a showdown in the U.S. presidential election.
我想美國總統選舉都有最後關鍵的時刻。

- There was a showdown between Republicans and Democratics in Congress.
  在國會裡共和黨和民主黨有摩擦。

- U.S. politicians should try to prevent showdowns among nations.
  美國政客應該避免與其他國家的敵對。

- The negotiator will be expected to face a showdown in China.
  談判者在中國將最後一次攤牌。

- Sooner or later there will be a showdown between the U.S. & Mexico.
  美國和墨西哥遲早都會攤牌。

sidekick

🔊 156

名詞 指常常與某人在一起，十分要好，男或女的密友（very good friend, male or female, by one's side all the time）

- Mr. Chang has been my sidekick for over twenty years.
  張先生是我廿年的好友。

- She has only one sidekick.
  她只有一位密友。（可指男或女）

嚴格來說，密友通常只有一位，故很少用複數，但現在很多人還是照用複數不誤。所以可以說：

- Many of his sidekicks attended his birthday party.
  他很多好友參加他的慶生會。

- In the past he had several sidekicks.
  過去他有數位好友。

有時也指一些同流合污，共同犯罪的密友。

例句

· They are sidekicks in crime.
（sidekicks = companions）

sine qua non

◀)) 157

拉丁文，指一種主要因素或必要的（absolutely necessary or essential）（當名詞）

例句

· A diploma has become a sine qua non for finding a decent job.
文憑成為取得像樣工作的必要條件。

· The ability to exchange ideas with others is a sine qua non of the scholarly life.
能與他人交換思想的能力，是學術生活必要的因素。

skyrocketing

◀)) 158

這個現在分詞當形容詞，意思是物價方面快速升高（anything goes up quickly, particularly refer to high prices because of inflation）

例句

· The skyrocketing price of gasoline has forced many Americans to cut back their long-distance trips.
汽油的猛漲使很多美國人減少長途的旅行。

· 或 The skyrocketing prices have forced her to cut back in her purchases.
物價的波動使她減少購買。

---

 skyrocket：就是猛升或猛漲，就像火箭式的上升。

例句

· The crime rate is skyrocketing in this area.
這個地區的犯罪率正在快速的升高。

· Medical costs in the U.S. are skyrocketing.
美國的醫藥費用正在猛升。

· His stocks have skyrocketed in the past two years.
過去兩年中，他的股票漲得很多。

· Because of his popular book, Mr. A has skyrocketed to fame.
由於他的暢銷書，A 先生一舉成名。

---

 skyrocket：原意是沖天火箭

例句

· Did China send up its first skyrocket a hundred years ago?
中國是在一百年前發射第一枚沖天火箭嗎？

soul-searching

 159

名詞 意思是深刻反省或憑良心自我深思（seeking true feeling in oneself or deep thinking）尤其在動機和價值方面（exam one's conscience over motive or value）

例句

· He needs to do more soul-searching.
他需要更多的深思。

· There was an intense soul-searching among us.
我們彼此間要深刻反省。

· His sudden decision shook many friends and provoked soul-searching with the group.
他突然的決定，驚動很多朋友，也使那群人深深的思考。

動詞 照理應該是：search the soul，可是很多人仍然使用 soul-search

例句

· He needs to soul-search to discover what occupation he would like to pursue.
他要深深考慮究竟要幹什麼工作。
（soul-search = search the soul）

· When it comes to the abortion issue, many people soul-search their positions.
一旦談到墮胎問題，很多人就要深深思考他們的立場。

也就是：
· Many people do a lot of soul-searching about abortion.

status quo

◀) 160

拉丁文，當名詞，指保持現狀或不變的狀況（actually existing）

例句

· Many people believe that Taiwan will maintain the status quo.
很多人認為台灣可以維持現狀。

· Are you satisfied with the status quo of our economy today?
你對目前不變的經濟狀況，感到滿意嗎？

stigma

◀) 161

 這個名詞，出自拉丁文，是指由於個人的原因而留下的汙點或恥辱（a mark or scar of disgrace）

例句

· Mr. Chen will not be able to escape the stigma arising from his actions.
由於陳先生的行為，他無法清除留下的汙名。

· Often the stigma seems more difficult to deal with than the event itself.
常常恥辱比事情的本身，似乎更難處理。

動詞 stigmatize，就是蒙受恥辱

- Mr. A's (sex) scandal may have stigmatized his respected family.
  A 先生的醜聞，使他受人尊敬的家庭，蒙受汙點。

tete-a-tete

🔊 162

法文，（發音 tatetat），指兩人面對面的私下會談或密談（a face-to-face private talk; or a confidential meeting between two persons）（當名詞）

例句

- President Obama and his advisor had a tete-a-tete on Chinese foreign policy.
  歐巴馬總統和他顧問密談對中國的外交政策。

- The two leaders had a friendly tete-a-tete by the fireplace.
  兩位領導人在火爐邊有次友好的私下會談。

ultimatum

🔊 163

名詞 意思是最後通牒（a final demand or offer）

例句

- The company issued an ultimatum to Mr. A demanding his resignation by next month.
  公司對 A 先生發出最後通牒，要他下月前辭職。

- Due to his infidelity, his wife has given him an ultimatum of divorce.
由於他的不貞行為，他妻子給他一個離婚的最後通牒。

- China may not issue an ultimatum for the reunification with Taiwan.
中國也許不會發出最後通牒要與台灣統一。

versatile

◀) 164

 意思是多才多藝或多功能（competent in many things; adaptable to many uses）

 例句

- Many readers consider Miss Chang a versatile writer.
許多讀者認為張小姐是位多才多藝的作家。

- We bought a versatile machine for making bread.
我們買了一部多功能的製麵包機

名詞 versatility

例句

- I always feel that Mr. A has been a painter of versatility.
我常覺得 A 先生是位多才多藝的畫家。

vindictive

🔊 165

 意思是報復性的，懷恨的（revengeful in spirit; said in revenge）

名詞 vindictiveness

例句

· Any vindictive acts toward this issue will not do any good.
對這問題的任何報復性舉動，都無所補益。

· Do not create a vindictive spirit on Taiwan-China relations.
對中台關係，不可製造惡意的氣氛。

· His vindictiveness to her is unlikely to be changed.
他對她的懷恨，不太可能會改變。

windfall

🔊 166

名詞 指意外之財，也就是意外獲得一件東西或很快得到一筆巨款（get a large amount of money quickly or unexpectedly）

例句

· Our school has received a windfall from a wealthy alumnus.
我們學校意外收到一筆來自校友的捐款。

· He wishes a windfall might come his way.
他盼望能得到一筆意外的巨款。

· Many people hope to have a lottery windfall.
很多人都希望得到彩券的橫財。

· Mr. A expects a windfall profit from playing the stock market.
A 先生期待玩股票能得到一筆意外的利潤。

但照字義，也指被風吹落的果子。

例句

· The grass of the orchard was covered with a windfall.
果園的草地落了一顆果子。

youthhostel

 167

名詞 指年輕人騎單車旅行膳宿的地方（a place for young people to stay on bike traveling）這些地方，多半是大學，利用暑假開放，以最經濟實惠的方式為他們服務。
同理，在暑假中，供給老人各種旅遊活動的膳宿地方，稱為 elderhostel。

例句

· There are many youthhostels in the U.S.
在美國有很多供年輕人單車旅行膳宿的地方。

· Youthhostel or elderhostel programs have helped save traveling expenses for the young and the old.
提供年輕和年老人的簡便膳宿地方，節省他們許多的旅行費用。
（凡參加以上活動的人稱之為 youthhostler 和 elderhostler）

yuppie

 168

名詞 指那些事業有成，賺了很多錢的年輕男人或女人（young people, men or women, who do very well financially）（有人譯成雅痞）

例句

· Mr. Yeh has been considered a yuppie.
葉先生被認為是位有錢的年輕人。

· He always likes to have a yuppie lifestyle.
他喜歡過著有錢年輕人的生活方式。

· You are not wealthy, so don't try to portray yourself as a yuppie.
你並不富有，所以不要把自己裝成有錢的年輕人。

· Some people are jealous of yuppies.
有些人妒忌年輕有錢人。

注意：不可與 hippie（或 hippy）這個字弄混。（多數是 hippies）
hippie 是指過去一批衣著古怪，留著長髮，吸菸吸毒的嬉皮。

· In the 1960s, hippies were very prevalent.
六十年代嬉皮是很流行的。

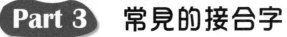

Part 3　常見的接合字

　　英文中，接合字的用法（hyphenation），除了字典中音節的劃分，常用在連接複合字（compound words）。

　　接合字在文法上沒有嚴格的規定，尤其美國人喜歡把接合字拼成一個字，或拆開來使用。現在許多美國人口語上或寫作時，找不到適當的字，就把幾個字用接合號（hyphen）連在一起，當作形容詞或名詞用，表示「不尋常」的味道（something unusual）或是「簡便的手法」（handy device）。

　　以下介紹一些常見的接合字（hyphenated words）。

Part 3　常用的接合字

back-to-back　🔊 169

 意思是繼續兩次

例句

· This is the first time that we have had a back-to-back winner.
我們繼續兩次勝利，還是第一回。

· Your back-to-back e-mails did not improve our mutual understanding.
你前後兩次的電子郵件，並沒有改善我們對彼此的了解。

back-to-basics　🔊 170

 指基本的原則、規律、訓練等

例句

· American education emphasizes a back-to-basics policy.
美國教育著重基本訓練。

· A back-to-basics religion appeals to some people.
宗教的基本規律對某些人有吸引力。（也就是指基要主義者 fundamentalist）

back-to-school

◀)) 171

形容詞 返校的季節

例句

· Back-to-school purchases may pinch many parents' budgets.
孩子返校時，要買各種物品，讓許多父母手頭拮据。
（動詞 pinch 是收縮或節制）

· There are many special sales during the back-to-school season.
學生返校季節，有許多特別減價。

be-all-and-end-all

◀)) 172

名詞 意思是最終目標或終結（final goal）

例句

· Money is not the be-all-and-end-all of my existence.
金錢不是我生存的最終目標。

形容詞 最終的

例句

· The be-all-and-end-all method to solve the problem is to negotiate and compromise with each other.
解決問題的最終方法是彼此的磋商與妥協。

· What will be the be-all-and-end-all to the Taiwan issue?
台灣問題的終結會是什麼呢？

behind-the-scene

🔊 173

 意思是在幕後，在後台或不公開，秘密的

例句

· The behind-the-scene decision may sometimes lead to the use of military force.
幕後秘密的決定，有些會導致使用軍事武力。
（也有人用 scenes）

副詞 在幕後

例句

· Many Chinese scientists in the U.S. work behind-the-scenes because of their language barrier.
許多在美的中國科學家，由於語言的障礙而在幕後工作。

bricks-and-mortar

🔊 174

---

 brick 是磚頭，mortar 是砂漿，也就是指房子等建築物。
（building of any kind）

例句

· All his money has been spent on bricks-and-mortar.
他的所有錢都花在房產上。

實體的

例句

· Some shoppers try to get off the Internet and (get) into bricks-and-mortar stores.
有些採購者想從網路上轉到真正的實體商店。

· Mr. A seems to be a bricks-and-mortar politician.
A 先生似乎是位著重房地產方面的政客。

bumper-to-bumper

 175

 意思是汽車一輛接一輛的（bumper 本是汽車後的保險桿）

例句

· During the holidays, some highways were jammed with bumper-to-bumper traffic.
假期時間，高速公路上的汽車一輛接一輛地堵塞。（也有人不用接合號）

· Bumper-to-bumper traffic may result in many people taking a longer time to reach a place.
交通堵塞造成許多人到達時間拖延。

catch-as-catch-can

🔊 176

形容詞 指能抓到什麼就抓什麼；隨便什麼辦法（whatever one can get）

例句

· Mr. Wang is leading a catch-as-catch-can life, working as a server at a restaurant.
靠在餐館當侍者的王先生，過著一種「能有什麼就幹什麼」的生活。

· Without command of the English language, many Chinese immigrants lead catch-as-catch-can lives.
許多沒有英語能力的老中移民，只能過著「隨便什麼工作都行」的日子。

· Mr. A appears to be satisfied with his catch-as-catch-can existence.
A 先生那種「流動臨時工湊合」的生存方式，似乎很滿足。

circle-the-wagons

🔊 177

形容詞 照字義就是把四輪車圈繞起來當防衛，也是形成一種防守或保衛（to form a defense）

例句

· Mr. B tries to carry out his policy from a circle-the-wagon position.
B 先生以一種防守立場，實行他的政策。

- Your circle-the-wagons attitude against this project has caused some inconvenience.
  你反對這計劃的防守態度，造成一些不便。

- Instead of circling-the-wagons, try to be more open!
  不必如此的防守，大方開闊些！（用動名詞 circling-the-wagon）
  （也就是：Don't be so defensive.）

do-everything-be-everywhere 🔊 178

 什麼事都去做，什麼地方也都去。

例句

- Mr. Ma's leadership style is do-everything-be-everywhere.
  馬先生的領導風格是「什麼都做」「那兒都去」。

- It is very tiresome for anyone to be a do-everything-be-everywhere person.
  一位「什麼都做」「那兒都去」的人，是蠻累的。

don't-ask-don't-tell 🔊 179

 就是不問也不說

例句

- The company has issued a don't-ask-don't-tell policy to its employees.
  公司對其員工頒佈一項「不問不說」的政策。（修飾名詞 policy）

- To avoid infighting and backbiting, we better keep a don't-ask-don't-tell idea in mind.

  為了避免內部爭鬥和背後誹謗，我們最好保持「不問不說」的心態。

down-in-the-dumps

◀)) 180

 意思是感到沮喪或消沉（dumps 本是垃圾堆）

例句

- He is a down-in-the-dumps man seeking ways to get out of a slump.

  他是沮喪的人，想法走出陷坑。（slump 是陷落）

- After his business failure, Mr. A was down in the dumps.

  A 先生意失敗後，感到很消沈。（也有人不用接合號）

earlier-than-usual

◀)) 181

 這句話是由普通正常英語「自創」出來的結合字。意思是比平常早些發生（happen sooner than expected）

例句

- The earlier-than-usual arrival of daylight saving time may create potential hiccupping.

  夏令時間比往常早到，可能造成暫時性的干擾。

  （hiccup 打嗝或暫時停頓；過去式及過去分詞都是 hiccuped 或 hiccupped）（hiccuping 或 hiccupping = glitch 暫時干擾）

  （daylight saving = daylight saving time 指在夏季把時間減掉一小時）

- This year's earlier-than-usual snow caused problems for many farmers.
  今年下雪比想像來得早,造成許多農民的問題。
  (當形容詞,修飾 snow)

但是不加連字號就是一般英語。

- Some teens appear to become more mature earlier than usual.
  一些青少年比預料成熟得早。

first-come-first-serve

◀)) 182

 意思是先來先有,或捷足先登,也就是第一個到的,第一個得到服務。

例句

- The free tickets will be issued on a first-come-first-serve basis.
  免費入場券是先到先發給。(後面多半跟 basis)

- This office operates on a first-come-first-serve basis.
  這個辦公室的營業,是誰先到誰就先得到服務。

fly-off-the-shelf

◀)) 183

 指貨物賣得很快(to sell something very fast)

例句

- Flying-off-the-shelf books will certainly please the authors.
  書賣得很快會使作者開心。

- These best-selling items are flying-off-the-shelf.
  暢銷東西都賣得很快。

· Top quality merchandise is fly-off-the-shelf merchandise.
品質最好的貨物，也是出售最快的貨物。
（句尾重覆 merchandise 係加強語氣）

foot-and-mouth

◀） 184

 這是指動物的口蹄疫或豬流感

例句

· Some countries confirmed cases of foot-and-mouth disease last year.
去年一些國家確認有口蹄疫的事件發生。（disease 亦可省去當名詞用）

 口蹄疫或豬流感

例句

· Are you still concerned about foot-and-mouth?
你還擔心豬流感嗎？
注意：foot-in-mouth 係指說錯話或說話不得體。

foot-in-mouth

◀） 185

 指說錯話或說話不得體。
這是結合俚語：put one's foot in one's mouth 而來。

例句

· He gave her a foot-in-mouth comment on her family.
他對她家庭作出不得體的評論。

get-rich-quick

🔊 186

形容詞 想辦法很快贏利，變成富有（apparently quickly profitable）

例句

· The get-rich-quick scheme has made Mr. Chen very disappointed in the end.
「快速富有」的詭計，讓陳先生最後很失望。

· By all means Mr. B is trying to get rich quick.
B 先生盡其所能俾能達到「快速致富」。（如不用接字號，就是一般英語）

名詞 動名詞 getting-rich-quick 當做名詞

例句

· There is no getting-rich-quick through legal means.
沒有通過合法手段而能「即速致富」。

give-and-take

🔊 187

名詞 指有捨有得，也就是互諒互讓。

例句

· They finally reached an agreement after a lot of give-and-take.
經過許多的互諒互讓，他們最後達成協議。

想法互諒互讓

例句

· Many Chinese hope the give-and-take political negotiations between China and Taiwan will succeed.
許多老中希望中國與台灣的政治協商，能以互諒互讓，取得成功。

go-it-alone

🔊 188

 意思是我行我素，獨斷獨行，不聽他人意見。

例句

· Mr. Bush's go-it-alone attitude will make it harder for the world to support the U.S.
布希先生的獨斷獨行態度，使國際支持美國，更為困難。

· A go-it-alone personality sometimes causes discord in relationships.
我行我素的性格，有時造成關係不調諧。

hand-me-down

🔊 189

 指別人用過的舊物或舊衣（the used stuff or clothes）

例句

· Many Americans accept hand-me-down clothes for their kids.
許多老美接受舊衣服給他們的孩子。

- Some Chinese consider a hand-me-down gift as a kind of insult.
  一些老中覺得用過的禮物是種侮辱。

 舊物或舊衣（可用複數）

例句

- I used to wear my elder brother's hand-me-downs.
  我過去穿用我哥哥的舊衣。

head-in-the-sand

◀)) 190

 意思是不正視事實；逃避現實，也就是採取鴕鳥政策（try not to face reality; unpractical）
這是從 to bury one's head in the sand 而來 = to play ostrich and pretend not to see 想學鴕鳥只當沒看見

例句

- The head-in-the-sand approach will only make this matter worse.
  逃避現實的作法，只會使這事情惡化。

- Some politicians in Taiwan should not be head-in-the-sand toward the one China policy.
  一些台灣政客對一中政策不該逃避現實。

- Instead of being head-in-the-sand, many people feel (that) Taiwan needs to sign a peace agreement with China.
  為了避免不正視事實，許多人認為台灣該與中國簽定和平協定。

heart-to-heart

 191

形容詞　意思是非常誠懇的，至誠的

例句

· We had a big heart-to-heart discussion about how to raise our children.
關於如何教養我們的孩子，我們有次誠懇的討論。

· A hear-to-heart talk may help solve this problem.
一次至誠的談話，也許有助解決這個問題。

hit-or-miss

 192

形容詞　意思是無計劃的，隨便的或碰運氣的（unplanned or careless）

例句

· Mr. Lee is known for being a chancy and hit-or-miss person.
李先生是節儉、碰運氣而聞名的人。

· His business is unlikely to succeed because of his hit-or-miss attitude.
由於他蠻不在乎的態度，他的生意恐難成功。

· Drought and heat have made the crabbing season hit-or-miss in the bay.
乾旱和熱浪使海灣的螃蟹季節不能確定。

join-in or step-aside

 193

 意思是有時參加，有時離開；也就是說，有時支持，有時不支持。

例句

· Mr. Chen's attitude toward China Policy seems to be join-in or step-aside.
陳先生對中國政策表現「時合時離」的作風。

· Mr. Smith has a join-in or step-aside style of management.
Smith 先生有種「時好時壞」的管理方式。

know-it-all

 194

名詞 自以為無所不知（pretend to know all）

例句

· No offense, but I think you are a know-it-all.
別見怪，我想你是一位自以為無所不知的人。
（no offense 意思是沒有觸犯你的意思或並無惡意或別見怪）
（offense = offence）

· Many Chinese consider Ph.Ds as know-it-alls.
許多老中認為博士無所不知。
（當名詞用，故可用複數）

形容詞 自以為無所不知的人

例句

· In the U.S., If someone calls you a know-it-all person, it is certainly a left-handed compliment.
在美國如果有人稱你為「無所不知」的人，那絕對不是一種誠意的誇獎。（left-handed 指 insincere）

less-than-stellar ◄)) 195

 形容詞 照字義是比傑出差些，也就是不很傑出；普通的（not so outstanding; ordinary）（stellar 是傑出的）

例句

· Mr. A's less-than-stellar ability to sell these products was expected.
A 先生銷售這些產品不很傑出的能力，是可預料的。

· Mr. B, even through less-than-stellar, has done a super job for his company.
B 先生，雖然不很傑出，但在公司工作超棒。

· Many who are less-than-stellar play important roles in our society.
許多普通常人在社會上扮演重要的角色。

live-and-let-live

 196

 意思是自己活，也要讓別人活；也就是互相寬容，和平共處或互不干擾的。

例句

· Mr. Nixon established a live-and-let-live policy of détente toward China.
尼克森先生對中國建立一個和平共處的政策。
（détente 是法文，意思是緩和國際緊張或和好。）

· We all should try hard to make this a live-and-let-live world.
我們大家必須為一個和平共處，互相寬容的世界而努力。
（由於這是一句流行的字眼，如果有人說成 live-and-let-die，當然就是開玩笑。）

make-or-break

◀)) 197

 意思是造成成功或失敗（to cause success or failure）

例句

· Weather is a make-or-break factor for many farmers.
氣候是許多農民成敗的因素。

· The leader of Taiwan is in a make-or-break position.
台灣領導人是處於成敗關鍵的地位。

· The one China policy can be a make-or-break proposition for some politicians in Taiwan.
一中政策對台灣某些政客而言，是關係成敗的論點。

matter-of-fact

 198

 意思是實事求是，切合實際。

例句

· As a pragmatist, Mr. J does everything in a matter-of-fact manner.
  J 先生是位實際主義者，做起事來，總是實事求是。

副詞 mater-of-factly 切合實際

例句

· He did try to deal with this problem matter-of-factly.
  他對處理這個問題，倒是切合實際。

middle-of-the-road

 199

形容詞 意思是溫和路線或中間立場。

例句

· China is taking a middle-of-the-road policy in its foreign affairs.
  中國的外交事務，採取溫和路線政策。

· Instead of helping either side, Mr. A would rather be middle-of-the-road.
  A 先生不幫任何一邊的忙，他寧可站在中間立場。

my-way-or-the-highway

 200

形容詞 照我意思做,否則就會被解僱(這裡的 highway,意味被解僱後,在馬路上開車回去)

例句

· The boss issued a my-way-or-the-highway statement to his employees.
老闆對他員工頒發「照我的話去做,不然就滾蛋」的聲明。

· Don't complain or you will lose your job because of the my-way-or-the-highway policy.
由於「不聽話,就滾蛋」的政策,還是不要埋怨,否則你會失去工作。

never-before-seen

 201

形容詞 意思是不尋常的

例句

· Mr. B is a type of never-before-seen person in my department.
在我的部門,B 先生是位不平常的人物。(可以指好或不好)

· A never-before-seen strain of swine flu has turned killer in Mexico.
一場不尋常而極度緊張的豬流感在墨西哥成為致命的疾病。

nickel-and-dime

🔊 202

形容詞 nickel 是美國硬幣五分，dime 是一毛，也就是少量的錢，或節省每個銅板，斤斤計較。

例句

· Mr. A seems to be a nickel-and-dime bidder in auction.
A 先生在拍賣場是位以少量錢出價的人。

· Raising the fines 25 cents each time is only a nickel-and-dime approach.
每次收取兩毛五的罰款，僅僅是小小數目的方式。

動詞 斤斤計較

例句

· Mr. Wang has been nickeled-and-dimed by his lawyer.
王先生的律師，一點一滴都要收費。
（也有人用 nickel-and-diming 當形容詞）

not-so-good

🔊 203

形容詞 不怎麼好

例句

· We should support each other in not-so-good times.
我們在「不怎麼好」的時候，應該互相支持。
（但通常不用 not-so-bad）

- Sometimes, China and the U.S. have to deal with their not-so-good relations.
中美兩國有時要處理「不怎麼好」的關係。

not-too-bad

◀) 204

 意思是還不錯,不很差

例句

- Finally, Mr. Chen has become a not-too-bad engineer.
最後陳先生成為一位還算不錯的工程師。

- Although he is not a top-notch teacher, he is a not-too-bad person.
雖然他不是第一流的老師,他還是不錯的人。

not-so-well-kept

◀) 205

 指不會好好收拾、保養或守住(do not take good care)

例句

- I went to a not-so-well-kept store yesterday.
昨天我去一家整理不怎麼好的商店。

- He will be unable to ask a good price for his not-so-well-kept house.
他沒有好好保養的房子,賣不到好的價錢。

· Mr. A's not-so-well-kept secret makes his friends know he has a terminal illness.
A 先生不太會守住秘密，使他朋友知道他得了絕症。

off-the-cuff

◀)) 206

 意思是未經準備的，隨意的，非正式的

例句

· Mr. A landed in some hot water with an off-the-cuff comment regarding this matter.
A 先生對這件事的隨意評論，惹上一些麻煩。（in hot water 是陷入困境）

· His off-the-cuff complaints have gotten on his coworkers' nerves.
他隨便埋怨，使他的同仁厭煩。
（to get on someone's nerve 是令人厭煩）（也有人不用接合號）

on-again-off-again

◀)) 207

 斷斷續續地（not continuously）

例句

· After three years of an on-again-off-again romance, she decided to marry him.
三年來斷斷續續的戀愛後，她決定嫁給他。

- The on-again-off-again relationship between China and U.S. seems to work out fine.
  中美兩國時好時壞的關係，進展得似乎還可以。

- Lucy does not know if she should break up her on-again-off-again life with her boyfriend.
  Lucy 不知是否要與斷斷續續生活一起的男友分開。

once-in-a-lifetime

🔊 208

 意思是一生中只有一次

例句

- You have to try harder; this is a once-in-a-lifetime opportunity.
  你要加倍努力；這是一生只有一次的機會。

- I will never forget what happened because it was a once-in-a-lifetime experience.
  我永遠不會忘記所發生的一切，因為那是生平唯一的經驗。
  （因為 once 的 o 讀為 w 音，所以前面冠詞用 a，不用 an）

once-over-lightly

🔊 209

 意思是做事很草率，很隨便或表面化（do something carelessly or superficially）

例句

- Some medical doctors give once-over-lightly treatments to their patients.
  有些醫師對他們病人的治療很草率。

- Sometimes the reporters provide a once-over-lightly coverage of certain news.
  有時候記者對某些新聞只做表面的報導。

- Your once-over-lightly attitude in performing the project may lead to its failure.
  你執行計劃的隨便態度，也許會導致失敗。

once-upon-a-time

🔊 210

形容詞　指優美無比的或像童話般的奇景

例句

- To recapture our city's once-upon-a-time look, we see the need to restore the old buildings.
  為了重新捕捉先前都市的優美景色，我們需要整修舊的建築物。
  （修飾名詞 look）

- Visiting Disneyland is a once-upon-a-time experience.
  參觀迪斯尼樂園是個童話般美好的經驗。

one-of-a-kind

🔊 211

形容詞　意思是非常特別

例句

- To me, living on the shoreline seems to be a one-of-a-kind experience.
  對我來說，住在海岸線地帶似乎是特別的經驗。

- Mr. A, with his superior knowledge of English, is a one-of-a-kind professor.

A 先生有優越的英語知識，是位非常特別的教授。

one-size-fits-all

🔊 212

 本意是一個尺碼適合於所有身材的大小；或一個方法能解決許多問題。

例句

- His wife bought a one-size-fits-all bathrobe.

他太太買了一件一個尺碼適合所有身材的睡袍。（修飾 bathrobe）

- Frankly speaking, there is no one-size-fits-all answer to her problems.

老實說，沒有一個方法能解決她的問題。（修飾 answer）

one-to-one (basis)

🔊 213

意思是以個體為基礎，或一對一為根據。

例句

- Prejudice has prevented many people from getting to know African Americans on a one-to-one basis.

偏見阻止了許多人不以個體為單位去瞭解黑人。（指人時，也有人用 one-on-one basis）

- Don't generalize about any race; it should be judged on a one-to-one basis.

對任何種族不可籠統化或一概而論，要以個體為單位去瞭解別人。（後面通常跟 basis）

此外，如同：farm-to-market-road
· A farm-to-market-road fund needs to be appropriated.
從農場到市場的馬路基金，需要撥款。

out-of-pocket

🔊 214

 意思是自掏腰包或現金支付（to pay with your own money）

例句

· Cutting the pills and taking half doses may reduce patients' out-of-pocket prescription costs.
把藥片切成一半服用，也許能減少病人處方藥的開支。

· Generally speaking, food expenses are out-of-pocket.
一般而言，食品開支是現金支付的。

· The boy's out-of-pocket expenses are considerable.
這男孩的現金開銷是蠻大的。

out-of-the-way

🔊 215

 指荒僻的，罕見的，不尋常的（seldom seen; not often or unusual）

例句

· Mr. A's out-of-the-way remarks on this issue have made some people upset.
A 先生對這問題不得體的評論，造成一些人不高興。

- There is an out-of-the-way roadside restaurant near the river.
  靠近河邊的荒僻路旁有個餐館。

- Sometimes we can find an out-of-the-way item in a yard sale.
  我們有時在庭院買賣時找到不尋常的東西。

pie-in-the-face

🔊 216

 把「派」扣在臉上，這是老美一種開玩笑，表示輕微的「處分」。

例句

- He feels the pie-in-the-face custom should have been retired 50 years ago.
  他認為把「派」扣在臉上的習俗，50 年前就該休止。

- What an unpleasant experience it would be if I got the pie-in-the-face treatment!
  假如我受到扣「派」在臉上的待遇，那是多麼不愉快的經驗！

 許多人照音把 pie 譯成「派」，本是一種帶有奶油的餡餅，多半對明星、歌星等名人開玩笑

例句

- It seems silly to have a pie-in-the-face for a celebrity.
  把「派」扣在名人臉上，似乎很無聊。

play-by-play

 217

形容詞 通常用在 sports 方面，意思是每場比賽的實況報導，或詳盡敘述

例句

· Since you were not present at the scene, I would like to give you a play-by-play account.
由於你不在現場，我要給你詳盡敘述。

· Regarding this issue, you have to make a play-by-play report to your boss.
關於這件事，你要向你的上司做詳情報告。）
（也有美國人不用 hyphen）

point-and-shoot

 218

形容詞 本是指迅速照相，這裡意思是快速（fast or quick）

例句

· Mr. B is known for being a point-and-shoot negotiator.
B 先生因談判快速而聞名。

· A good speech should not be just point-and-shoot.
好的演講不只是匆忙快速的結束。

· Many people feel that to write point-and-shoot sentences is better than lengthy and complicated ones.
許多人認為快速簡短的句子要比冗長複雜的好些。

publish-or-perish

🔊 219

 意思是沒有著作，就會完蛋。（這是指大學教師，如果沒有什麼作品發表，就會被校方解聘。）

例句

· The publish-or-perish syndrome is prevalent in the U.S. academic world.
在美國學術界，「沒著作，就完蛋」是很普遍的現象。

· Many American college professors are concerned about a publish-or-perish policy.
許多美國大學教師為「沒著作，就完蛋」的政策而擔心。

rags-to-riches

🔊 220

 rag 本是破布；就是從貧窮到巨富（from being poor to rich）

例句

· Mr. B's interest in China is fueled by the rags-to-riches stories of young entrepreneurs.
有關年輕企業家從赤貧到巨富的故事，激起了 B 先生對中國的興趣。（fuel 是加油或激起）

· Through her jackpot winnings, Mary became a rags-to-riches woman.
Mary 中了彩券大獎後，從貧苦成為富有的女子。

· After his rags-to-riches rise, Mr. Wang bought a two-million-dollar mansion.
王先生由貧窮到富有後，買了兩戶百萬豪宅。
（rise 這裡是名詞，指地位的升高或興起）

 **ready-to-wear** 🔊 221

 現成的

例句

· You can find a scarf in the ready-to-wear department.
你可以在現成服裝部買到圍巾。

right-about-face 🔊 222

名詞 意思是一百八十度的轉向或徹底的改變

例句

· No one knows if the President will make a right-about-face on health care.
沒有人知道總統對健保是否會做一百八十度的轉變。
（= right-about-turn）

· What if the leader of Taiwan does a right-about-turn on China policy?
假如台灣領導人對中國政策作徹底的改變，那該怎麼辦？

right-of-center 🔊 223

 指偏右的；反之，left-of-center 是指偏左的

例句

· Mr. A is a right-of-center person while his wife is left-of-center.
A 先生是右派的人，但他的夫人是左派。

- There are always some right-of-center and some left-of-center voters in politics.

  在政治上，總是有些右派和左派的投票人。（也有人不用接合號）

round-the-clock

◀)) 224

 指一天 24 小時，一星期七天；或日夜不停，連續一整天。不過現代許多人的說法是 24/7。（24/7 讀成：twenty four seven）

例句

- Some stores offer a round-the-clock service.

  有些店鋪營業時間是一週七天，每天 24 小時。

- Las Vegas is the city that goes 24/7.

  拉斯維加斯是個不分日夜的城市。

round-the-world

◀)) 225

 意思是環繞世界

例句

- Mrs. Lin will take a round-the-world trip next year.

  林太太明年要環遊世界旅行。

- A round-the-world journey can make the elderly very tired.

  一次環繞世界的旅遊，會使老人家十分疲倦的。（elderly 是形容詞，前面加 the，是表示一般老年人。）

run-of-the-mill

🔊 226

形容詞 意思是一般性；普通的

例句

· Mr. A's job as the committee chairman has become a run-of-the-mill one.
A 先生擔任委員會的主席職位，已經成為一般性的工作。（one 指 job）

· Will you consider this problem as special or run-of-the-mill?
你認為這個問題是特殊的還是普通的？

So-and-So

🔊 227

名詞 意思是某某人

例句

· He complained that Mr. So-and-So was very arrogant at the meeting.
他埋怨某某先生在開會時很傲慢。（也可寫成 so-and-so）
（不願說出他是誰，也許是 Mr. Smith，或 Mr. Jones 或 Mr. Chen 等。）

· The woman said so-and-so bought a new car and she wanted to buy one, too.
這位女士說某某買了一部新車，她也要買一部。（只是指 someone）

但是如果說：
- Mr. Jones is a so-and-so.
（這裡的 so-and-so，是指不禮貌的字，或是罵人的 SOB，但又不願意用，以免有失自己身份等。）

soon-to-be

◄》228

 很快成為；很快就是

例句

- The soon-to-be ex-chairperson has vented some of his frustration at the outcome.
  他即將成為前任主席，在最後發洩他一些失意牢騷。

- The council members asked the soon-to-be mayor about his perspective of the city.
  議會委員們詢問即將上任的市長有關他對市政的展望。

standing-room-only

◄》229

 指座位都滿了，只有站立空間（People can only stand because there are no more seats.）

例句

- This discussion on the prevention of cancer has drawn standing-room-only crowds.
  這場預防癌症討論會，引來一大群聽眾，只剩站立空間了。

· Dr. B's speech on parenting created a standing-room-only audience.
B 醫師的教養子女演講，吸引大批聽眾，只剩站立空間了。

 坐無虛席（動名詞片語當名詞）

例句

· Almost 500 people turned out, with standing-room-only, for Mr. A's business celebration.
A 先生的商務慶祝，出席約有 500 人，坐無虛席，只有站立空間。

stay-the-course

🔊 230

 意思是奮力貫徹始終或堅持到底（stick to the end）

例句

· Mr. Bush used to rebuff critics of his stay-the-course strategy for his unpopular war in Iraq.
Bush 先生過去斷然拒絕對他不得人心而堅持到底的伊拉克戰爭策略所做的批評。

· Your stay-the-course efforts in this project will come to realization.
你對這個計劃貫徹始終的努力，將會實現。

動詞

· Some politicians will want to stay-the-course in Taiwan independence.
一些政客為台獨奮力貫徹始終。
（這裡 stay-the-course 是動詞片語，當一個字看待，也有人不用連字號）

stick-in-the-mud

名詞 指固執不求改變的人或不熱心,很保守

例句

· Don't be such a stick-in-the-mud.
不要做個固執不求改變的人。

形容詞 不熱心

例句

· They are too stick-in-the-mud about your idea.
他們對你的想法,不太熱心。

stickler-for-detail

名詞 指一切按照決定,十分注意細節(follow the rules exactly; pay close attention to trivial matter)

例句

· Having known Mr. A for two years, I have found him to be a stickler-for-detail.
認識 A 先生兩年來,我發覺他是位堅守規則重視細節的人。

· Some people are known for being sticklers-for-detail.
有些人是因按規辦事小心細節而聞名。(可用複數 sticklers)

· A stickler-for-detail is unlikely to please everybody.
固執己見,爭執瑣事的人,不太可能使人人高興。

形容詞

例句

· Do you think Ed is a stickler-for-detail inspector?
你認為 Ed 是重視細節的督察員嗎？

texting-while-driving

◀》 233

 形容詞　指開車時傳電子短訊（send message electronically during driving）

例句

· The state's texting-while-driving law is to be enforced.
州政府對開車時傳送電子訊息的法律將要加強。

· Stop the texting-while-driving habit; it is risky.
開車時不可傳電子短訊，那很危險。

 名詞

例句

· Texting-while-driving appears quite common among teenagers.
青少年開車時傳電子短訊，似乎很平常。

tit-for-tat

◀》 234

 形容詞　意思是以牙還牙，或針鋒相對。

例句

· Mr. A used a tit-for-tat response to his friend's verbal attack.
A 先生對朋友的口頭攻擊，採取以牙還牙的回應。

- Many politicians use tit-for-tat tactics in their campaigns.
許多政客在競選時採用針鋒相對的策略。

to-do-list

 235

 名詞 意思是列出要做的事情

例句

- Mr. Bush has given the Congress a to-do-list.
布希先生已經給國會列出要做的事情。

- After his retirement, he has many to-do-lists.
他退休後,列出許多要做的事情。

toe-to-toe

 236

 副詞 意思是面對面,非常靠近,有爭論的意味。

例句

- We can go toe-to-toe with him on personal safety.
對個人安全方面,我們可以與他面對面磋商。

 形容詞

例句

- A Toe-to-toe dispute will not improve the situation.
面對面的爭執,並不能改善情況。

tongue-in-cheek 🔊 237

 指無誠意，偽意或挖苦的（not sincere）

例句

- Mr. A's tongue-in-cheek comments about his boss seemed inappropriate.
  A 先生對他老闆挖苦的評論，不很恰當。

- What Bob has told me appears to be tongue-in-cheek.
  Bob 對我所說的似乎不誠懇。

- A tongue-in-cheek person is unlikely to be trusted.
  一位偽情偽意的人，不太被人信任。

too-tight (clothing or jeans) 🔊 238

 意思是穿緊身的衣服或牛仔褲等

例句

- The young woman dressed in too-tight jeans and wore extremely low-cut tops.
  這位年輕的姑娘穿著很緊的牛仔褲和非常低胸的上衣。

- His wife has a sexy figure; she loves to wear too-tight clothing to show it off.
  他老婆身材很性感；她喜歡穿緊身衣服顯露一番。

- 但如果說：Mr. Chen is always too-tight.（或 too tight）
  陳先生很小氣吝嗇。
  （這裡的 too-tight = tightwad = cheapskate）

top-of-the-line

◀)) 239

 指最貴的,最豪華的

例句

· Mr. A bought some high-end clothing and top-of-the-line shoes.
  A 先生買了一些高檔的衣服和昂貴的鞋子。

· To show off his wealth, Mr. B always chooses a top-of-the-line sports car.
  B 先生為了炫耀富有,常常選用名貴的跑車。

trial-and-error

◀)) 240

 試錯法,這是美國心理學家 E. L. Thorndike 的理論,他認為人類學習是通過嘗試錯誤的過程。(try and expect to make an error)

例句

· The trial-and-error theory has been accepted by worldwide educators.
  試錯法理論已受到世界性教育家的接受。

 試錯法

例句

· This is a trial-and-error for children and adult as well.
  這是一種孩子和成人都能使用的「由犯錯而取得經驗」的方法。

- Don't be afraid of making mistakes; a trial-and-error can be valuable.

  不必害怕犯錯；試錯法很有價值。

two-pack-a-day

🔊 241

 這是指一天吸兩包香菸的人或習慣

- Being a chain smoker, Mr. Wang has a two-pack-a-day (cigarette) habit.

  做為一位菸鬼，王先生有一天吸兩包的習慣。（ cigarette 可省去）

- A person with a two-pack-a-day (smoking) habit may develop lung cancer.

  一天吸兩包香菸的人，可能會得肺癌。（ smoking 可省去）

  （當然可以說：每天三包、四包、五包，但多半只說一天兩包。）

two-way street

🔊 242

名詞　本意是「雙向道」，但這裡是指雙方面的，互相的，彼此的。

例句

- Friendship is always a two-way street.

  友誼都是要雙方面的。

- Of course, I believe free trade is also a two-way street.

  當然，我相信自由貿易也是雙方面的。

但是 one-way street，倒是真正指「單行道」，不過也可用在否定句。

例句

· Love or friendship is certainly not a one-way street.
愛情或友誼絕非單方面的。
（因為 two-way street 是很流行的說法，如果有人說成 three-way street，當然就是開玩笑了。）

use-it-or-lose-it

🔊 243

 不用它就會失去它（if you don't use it, you'll lose it）

例句

· Some organizations have a use-it-or-lose-it policy on employees' annual leave.
有些機構對員工的年假採取「不用就失去」的政策。

· It is a use-it-or-lose-it opportunity for him to accept the offer.
對他來說，這是一次「不接受就失去」的機會。

名詞 指一種「不利用就失去」的思想或觀念

例句

· Use-it-or-lose-it has created a dilemma for Mrs. Wang.
「不利用就失去」的想法，使得王太太進退兩難。

take-it-or-leave-it

 244

形容詞 指一種磋商，只有一種選擇

例句

· A take-it-or-leave-it sales attitude is not highly recommended.
「要就拿，不要就拉倒」的銷售態度，不是高度受人讚賞的。

· The negotiator always sticks to a fixed policy and take-it-or-leave-it manner.
這位談判者，堅守固定政策，並採用「要就這樣，否則就算了」的態度。

· This is your decision; (you) take it or (you) leave it.
這是你的決定，取捨由你。（就成為一般英語用法了）
（you 被省去）

wash-and-wear

 245

形容詞 免燙的

例句

· Nowadays, many clothes are made with wash-and-wear materials.
現在很多衣衫的材料都是免燙的。

· Wash-and-wear clothing may have taken a heavy toll of the laundry business.
免燙的衣服對洗衣業造成很大的影響。
（to take a heavy toll 是造成重大傷害或損失）

wolf-in-sheep's-clothing

 指壞人偽裝好人，也就是披著羊皮的狼（a bad guy pretends to be a good one）

例句

· Mr. Chen's wolf-in-sheep's-clothing policy has already come to light.
陳先生「偽裝好人」的策略，已經水落石出。
（come to light 為人所知）

· No one will trust a person proven to be a wolf-in-sheep's-clothing.
沒有人會相信一位已證實的「偽裝好人」。

· A wolf-in-sheep's-clothing politician should not be allowed to run for office.
偽裝好人的政客，不該允許擔任公職。

word-of-mouth

 意思由口頭傳開（spread by talking）

例句

· In spite of modern technology, we still live in a word-of-mouth society.
儘管現代的科技，我們仍然活在由口傳話的社會。

· Sometimes a word-of-mouth method is more effective than advertisements.
有時候，由口碑相傳還比廣告有效。

例句

· Bad news spreads faster by word-of-mouth.
壞消息從口傳開更快。

183

Note

Part 4 辨別容易混淆的字詞

　　學習英文時，常常遇到許多「容易令人混淆」的單字，有的意義相近，有的用法迥異但拼法接近，諸如 lie / lay、sit / set、rise / raise 三組動詞，就非常令人「頭痛」，也有一些字，在字尾加上 r 或 er，或是加上 e 或 ee 就產生不同的變化。

　　以下將經常容易弄錯的單字，舉例加以詳加說明。

Part 4　辨別容易混淆字詞

▶▶ lie 與 lay

🔊 248

---

lie：意思是躺下休息或位於（recline to rest or to be situated），表示人、地、物的位置。因為它是不及物動詞（intransitive verb），所以後面不能有受詞，也不能有被動語態；通常用副詞或介詞片語當副詞去修飾。（動詞時態：lie, lay, lain, lying）

---

lay：意思是把某件東西放下，或置某件東西於某處（to put something down or to place something somewhere）。因為它是及物動詞（transitive verb）所以後面有受詞，也可用在被動語態（passive voice）（動詞時態：lay, laid, laid, laying）

例句

· Mr. Wang usually lies down for a nap after lunch.
王先生通常午餐後躺下小睡一會。

· Yesterday I lay on the sofa listening to classical music.
昨天我躺在沙發上聽古典音樂。

· The girl has lain on the beach for an hour.
女孩躺在沙灘上一小時了。

· Mr. Chang was lying on the couch reading a novel.
張先生躺在沙發上看小說。

· The new area was rug lying in front of the kitchen.
廚房前放了一塊新地毯。
（area rug 是指裝飾用的小塊地毯）

- A small temple once lay somewhere in the hill.
  在山丘的某處，曾經有座小廟。
  （因為意味小廟現在可能不存在，所以可用過去式 lay）

- The secret of his success lies in his hardwork.
  他的成功在於他的努力。

- Mrs. Lin always lays a wool blanket on her bed.
  林太太常在床上放一床毛毯。（lays = puts）

- Yesterday I laid some books on my desk.
  昨天我在我的書桌上放了幾本書。（laid = put）

- Someone had laid the wet sheet over the sofa.
  有人把濕被單鋪在沙發上。（had laid = had put）

- The workers are laying a new carpet on the floor.
  工人在地板上鋪新地毯。

註：及物動詞後面很少跟間接受詞。如果說：The workers are laying us a new carpet on the floor. 這時，間接受詞是 us，顯得十分勉強。至於被動語態，老外也很少使用。假如說：A new carpet is being laid on the floor by the workers. 不如主動語態顯得簡單而有力。

注意：
lie 如果指說謊（to tell a falsehood），其動詞時態是：lie, lied, lied, lying

例句

- Do not lie to others.
  不要對他人說謊。

- Mr. A has often lied to his wife.
  A 先生常對他太太說謊。

・Are you lying to your boss？
你在對老闆說謊嗎？

》 sit 與 set

---

sit：不及物動詞，意思是坐下或座落於（**to take a seat or to be located**）所以後面沒有受詞，也不能有被動語態，多半用副詞或介詞片語當副詞去修飾。（動詞時態是：**sit, sat, sat, sitting**）

---

set：是及物動詞，意思是放置某件東西（**to put or to place something**）後面有受詞，也可以有被動語態。（動詞時態是：**set, set, set, setting**）

例句

・His father always sits near the fireplace when he reads.
他老爸閱讀時，總是坐在壁爐邊。

・Mr. Wang likes to sit in the back of the classroom.
王先生喜歡坐在教室後面。

・Everyone will sit down when the company president says, "Be seated."
當公司總裁說「請坐」，大家都坐下。

・They were sitting there when I came.
我來時，他們正坐在那裡。

・Her grandfather has sat on the same couch for years.
她祖父多年來坐的是同樣的沙發。

・The statue sits on the top of（或 under the foot of）the mountain.
塑像坐落於山頂上（或山腳下）。

- Please set the dictionary on the top of the shelf.
  請把字典放在架子上。（set = put）

- His wife sets the coffee on the kitchen counter every morning.
  他太太每天早晨把咖啡放在廚房的台子上。

- The parents have set a date for their daughter's engagement.
  父母選定了他們女兒訂婚的日子。（have set = have fixed）

- In spring we will set the clock ahead one hour.
  春天我們將把時鐘撥快一小時。

- Some sellers have set the price(s) too high / steep.
  有些賣主把價格訂得太高。
  （以上例子，間接受詞和被動語態，較少使用）

»» rise 與 raise
◀)) 250

---

rise：意思是起身、起來或增加（to get up; to go up or to increase），這是不及物動詞，後面沒有受詞，而且不用被動語態，多半用副詞或介詞片語（或子句）當副詞去修飾。（動詞時態是：rise , rose , risen , rising）

---

raise：意思是舉起某件東西或增加數量（to lift up something or to increase the amount），這是及物動詞，後面有受詞，也可以有被動語態。（動詞時態是：raise , raised , raised , raising）

例句

- We all know that the sun rises in the east.
  我們都知道太陽從東邊上升。

- As she lifted the cover, the steam rose from the frying pan.
  當她拿起蓋子，炒鍋的蒸氣就上升了。（rose = went up）

· The assembly will rise when the judge enters the court room.
當法官走進法庭，與會者將全部起立。

· Mr. Wang has risen in his profession over the past five years.
過去五年中，王先生在他專業裡，步步高升。

· The speaker rose to address the graduates.
演講者起立，要向畢業生說話。

· Gasoline prices have been rising sharply（或 steadily）since
last month.
自上月起，汽油價格猛漲。（或持續上升）

· Please raise the window a little bit higher.
請把窗戶開高一點。

· There is no need for some Chinese to raise their voices.
一些中國人其實不必提高嗓門說話。

· Some students raised their hands when they asked questions.
一些學生舉手問問題。

· The landlore will raise the rent from this October.
自今年 10 月份起，房東將增加租金。

· The owner has raised the prices of merchandise in his store.
主人提高他店裡的貨品價格。

· Mr. A has been raising corn and vegetables on his farm.
A 先生在他田裡種玉米和蔬菜。

總之，要記得：lie , rise , sit 都是不及物動詞，後面沒有受詞，也
不能用被動。而 lay, raise , set 都是及物動詞，後面有受詞，也可
用被動。還要記得它們的時態變化。

⟫ like 與 as

🔊 251

---

like：通常當做介系詞用，意思是與什麼相似（similar to）或同樣的（in the same way），後面跟受詞（followed by an object）

---

as：多半當連接詞用，而且通常引用全句時使用，也就是用在主詞和動詞之前。

例句

· Sometimes using the rubbing alcohol feels like ice on my skin.
有時在皮膚上擦酒精就像冰一樣的冷。

· Great writers like Mark Twain only appear once in a blue moon.
像馬克吐溫那樣偉大的作家，是很罕見的。

· The soup that I ordered yesterday did not taste as it should.
昨天我叫的湯，味道好像不對勁。

· Your proposal worked just as you indicated it would.
你的提案，如你所說，可以行得通。

不過，as 有時也當介詞用，意思是相等或身分一致（equivalence or same identity）

例句

· After retirement, Mr. A works as a salesperson in a grocery store.
A 先生退休後，在一家雜貨店當銷貨員。
（Mr. A 即 salesperson）

»» abused 與 abusive 〔252

abused：指被人打罵虐待，這可能包括 verbal（語言上）, physical（肢體上）和 emotional（情緒上），這種人多係受害者（victim）

abusive：指常常喜歡吵鬧、打罵別人，也包括口頭上、身體上或感情上的虐待，不過這種人不是受害者

例句

· She is an abused wife.
　她是常被老公打罵的老婆。
= She was abused by her husband.

但是如果說：
· She is an abusive wife. 她是一位虐待老公的太太。
= She abuses her husband.

· Don't use abusive language!
　不可口出惡言！

· It is wise to remove yourself from an abusive environment.
　最好遠離被辱罵的環境。

至於 abuser 也是指喜歡辱罵別人者：
· Family abusers are condemned by our society.
　社會責難家庭中的虐待者。

»» accept 與 except 〔253

accept：當動詞用，意思是接受或同意（take what is offered; to agree to）

except：是介系詞，意思是除⋯⋯之外（leaving out; other than）

例句

· I willingly accepted the responsibility for the problem.
我願意為這問題承擔責任。

· Certainly, Mr. Chen will accept her invitation.
當然陳先生會接受她的邀請。

· Everyone except him attended the meeting.
除他之外，每個人都去參加開會。

· No one except you agrees to the idea of taking a trip to France.
除你之外，沒有人同意去法國旅行的念頭。

也可用在子句裡：

· This is a beautiful watch except that I don't have enough money to buy it.
這是一只漂亮的錶，只可惜我不夠錢買。

▶▶ activist 與 dissident

🔊 254

activist：指對社會某種理念或目標很活躍，對政府的政策也贊成，也反對，但未必是反政府的（to promote some particular cause, but not necessarily against government）

dissident：指異議分子，對政治或政府都是不滿和反對（always try to do something against government）

例句

· There are some Chinese dissidents in the U.S.
在美國有些反政府的中國異議分子。

· Several dissidents are considered (as) persona non grata by a certain government.
一些異議分子不受某一政府的歡迎。（即黑名單）
（單數是 persona non grata 是拉丁文，「受歡迎的」就是 persona grata）

· Environmental activists are trying to save the bay.
主張保護環境的激進分子設法拯救這個湖泊或海灣。

· He has been an activist for consumer's rights.
他是爭取消費者權益的活躍分子。

· Political activists would like to influence the presidential election.
政治的活躍分子想要影響總統的選舉。

· Should political activists（或 activism）be banned for social stability in China?
為了社會安定，中國應該禁止政治活躍分子嗎？
（activism：名詞，是指激進派的一種行為。）

 adoptive 與 adopted ◀》 255

---

adoptive：指領養別人的孩子

---

adopted：被收養的孩子
（動詞是 adopt，名詞是 adoption）

例句

· He will be an adoptive parent.
= He will get a child for adoption.

· The boy was an adopted son. = The boy was adopted. 或 He has an adopted child.

如果要強調是親生父母，則應該說：
· She is the birth mother.（不用 biological mother）
· He is her biological father.（不用 birth father）

≫ affect 與 effect
◀)) 256

affect：動詞，意思是影響或使改變（to influence or to bring about a change in）

effect：名詞，意思是結果（result）；當動詞用，意思是引起（to cause）

例句

· The cold weather has affected her skin allergy.
冷天氣影響到她皮膚過敏。

· Weather affects the farmer's income.
氣候會影響農夫的收入。

· What effect do you think we will have on the future plan?
你想將來計畫的結果是什麼呢？

· You will feel the effect of the medicine soon.
你很快就會感到藥物的效果。

· This change was effected by Mr. A's hard work.
這個改變，是因為 A 先生的努力而引起。（= caused）

allusion 與 illusion　　🔊 257

allusion：名詞，意思是暗指、影射或間接提到某人某事（indirect reference to someone or something）

illusion：名詞，指假象或一種幻想（a sort of fantasy）

例句

· In speaking it is better not to make any personal allusion about other person's character.
說話時，最好不影射他人的品格。

· Mr. B may get hurt by your allusion to his previous scandal.
你暗指 B 先生過去的醜聞，會令他難過。

· Although Mr. A has a heart problem, his ruddy complexion gives his friends the illusion of good health.
雖然 A 先生有心臟病，但他紅光滿面，給他朋友健康的假象。

· He feels some of Taiwan's politicians have an illusion that the U.S. will send troops to Taiwan for its independence.
他覺得台灣有些政客也許有個錯覺，認為美國會派兵支援台獨。

apprehend 與 comprehend　　🔊 258

apprehend：動詞，意思是逮捕或擔心（arrest or concern）

comprehend：動詞，意思是理解（understand）其名詞是 comprehension

例句

· The murderer was apprehended yesterday.
兇手昨天被捕。（apprehended = caughted = arrested）

- He has some apprehensions about the upcoming interview.
  他對即將來臨的面試，有些擔心。
  （通常用複數名詞 apprehensions）（= concern）

- The student comprehends English quickly.
  學生很快理解英語。

- She has quite a lot of comprehension about insurance.
  她對保險十分瞭解。（= understanding）

- With his teachers' assistance, he can comprehend math better.
  由於老師的幫助，他對數學理解較好。

≫ approve 與 agree　　　　　🔊 259

approve：通常所指的批准，具有合法的權威性或使某種事情合法化

approve of：多半是指好的一面，如結婚等。但 approve of 只是表示贊成或不贊成的意見，沒有使其合法的批准權力

agree：多半指對一個提議或計畫表示允諾或同意（可能是好或不好）

例句

- The legislature will have to approve gay marriage.
  立法機構必須批准同性戀結婚。（才能合法）

- Our school dean has approved her application.
  本校教務長批准了她的申請。（才能生效）

- At first, her parents did not approve of her marriage.
  （這裡用 approve of 是因為父母對兒女的婚姻，沒有批准的權力，只有表示贊成或不贊成的意見）

- I do not approve of my son's friendship with John.
  我不贊成兒子與 John 交朋友。（交友本是好事，但我有贊成或不贊成的意見）

· He does not approve of my tactics.
他不贊成我的策略。（也許我的策略不錯，但他可以不贊成）

· He agreed to the arrangements for our trip.
他同意我們旅行的安排。（未必是好安排，但他還是同意了）

· I agree with you now, but I may change my mind later.
我現在允諾你，但以後我可能改變主意。（也許現在只是勉強同意一下）

》 book-worm 與 book-learned　　◀) 260

book-worm（book worm）：名詞，多半指極愛讀書的人，尤其特別愛看小說（someone who loves fictions）但未必能把書本上的知識用到生活上，即所謂的「書呆子」、「書蟲」。這當然有點不恭之意。

book-learned：形容詞，通常是指愛讀較為專業的非小說書籍（someone who learns a lot through non-fiction），這種人，雖然缺乏實際經驗，但還能「學以致用」，勉強可稱為「活讀書」者。

例句

· In America, book-learned persons generally earn more respect than book worms (do).
在美國，活讀書的人，通常比書呆子受到尊敬。

· Mr. Chen is just another book worm.
陳先生只不過是個書呆子。
（book worm 後面不必加 person）

但如果說：
· Mr. A is a book-learned person.
  A 先生還算個能學以致用的人。
= Mr. A is book-learned.

· Are all people with Ph. D.s thought to be book-leaned?
  有博士學位的人，都能稱為「活讀書」的人嗎？

如果某人在專業上很有學識，就可以說：
· Mr. A is book-learned in computers.

但 book-learning 涵意不同
· He has book-learning.（或 book learning）
  （意味他有許多書本知識，但未必能應用在 real life 上。）

註：一般美國人十分重視讀書人的誠實、品格、道德，對學位不
    如中國人那麼看重；更沒有「萬般皆下品，唯有讀書高」的思
    想，所以他們對每種行業都較尊重，以提高敬業精神。

≫ bring 與 take   ◀)) 261

bring：指從遠處拿到近處（to carry from a farther place to a
nearer place），也就是說，動作是向著說話者而來（to show
movement toward the speaker）（動詞時態：bring, brought,
brought, bringing）

----

take：從近處拿到遠處（to carry from a nearer place to a
farther place），也就是指動作離開說話者而去（to show
movement away from the speaker）（動詞時態是：take, took,
taken, taking）

例句

· Don't bring all the problems to me.
不要帶給我許多問題。（動作向著說話者而來）

· Mr. A brought us some junk food.
A 先生帶給我們一些垃圾食物。（指速食等不健康的食物）（從遠處帶到近處）

· You may take this book with you.
你可以帶走這本書。（由近處帶到遠處）

· The teacher said, "John did not bring his books to school."
老師說：「John 沒有帶書來學校。」（對老師來說，學校較近，John 的家較遠。

· The mother said, "John did not take his books to school."
媽媽說：「John 沒有帶書去學校。」（對母親來說，家較近，學校較遠。

· Please take this letter to Mr. Wang and bring back a reply.
請把這封信帶給王先生，並帶回他的回音。

›› censor 與 censure　🔊 262

censor：動詞，指新聞、書報或電影等，對外發行前的審查（to exam a film , a writing , etc. before getting to the public）

censure：動詞，意思是責備、非難或指摘（to scold or condemn someone for wrongdoing）

例句

· Some governments will censor certain anti-policy newspapers.
有些政府要審查反政策的報紙。

- Any indecent advertisements need to be censored.
  任何粗鄙或有傷風化的廣告，應該刪去。

- Our school authorities censured Mr. A for his misconduct.
  我們學校當局責備 A 先生的不當行為。

- Mr. Wang has been censured for his tardiness at work.
  王先生上班遲到被批評。
  censorship：名詞，則指審查行為（act of censoring）

例句

- Press censorship is being carried out in many countries.
  許多國家實行新聞審查。（名詞）

有時 censure 也當名詞用。如：
- The committee calls for the censure of Mr. A.
  委員會要求對 A 先生公開譴責。（名詞）

» climate 與 weather �))) 263

climate：通常意義較廣，多指一般性較長的氣候或氣候區（long range condition in general; more broad and academic）

weather：指範圍較小，屬地方性的天氣（short period of time; local）

例句

- The climate of Taiwan is warmer than that of California.
  台灣氣候比加州熱。（指一般性，範圍較大。）

· The weather in Taiwan at this time of the year tends to be hot and humid.
這個時候台灣的天氣，可能是炎熱而潮濕。（指較短的時間，而且範圍較小。

不過也有一些老外把這兩個字交替使用

climate：也可指社會的風氣或潮流。

例句

· The moral climate in our society is declining.
我們社會的道德風氣節節下降。（climate = condition）

weather：當動詞用，有「度過難關」的意思。
例句

· The ship has weathered the storm.
船已度過暴風的難關。
（weather = last through，也就是 went through storm without serious damage or sinking）

» compensation 與 reparations   ◄» 264

compensation：名詞，指一般性的賠償（動詞是 compensate）

reparations：名詞，多半係指戰敗國須付的賠款（多用複數），這個字沒有動詞，多用 to make reparations 替代。

例句

· If Japan wants to be on good terms with China, she must make apologies and reparations to the Chinese people.
假如日本要與中國友好相處，她就必須向中國人民道歉和賠償。

- Should the Japanese government ignore making reparations for killing 35 million Chinese people?
殺害 3,500 萬中國人，日本政府可以漠視賠償嗎？

- The company will make compensation for the flood damage to his home.
公司將為他的房子受到水災損失而賠償。

- The injured worker asked the firm to compensate him for his time lost.（或 lost time）
受傷工人向公司要求賠償他時間的損失。

» complement 與 compliment　　　🔊 265

complement：動詞，意思是補充，使其完整（to complete or to make perfect）

compliment：動詞，是對某人的恭維（to say something good about a person）
（這兩個字，多半當動詞和名詞用。）

例句

- These building materials will complement those you already have.
這些建屋材料能補充你已有的材料。（動詞）

- Your part of the job complements mine.
你的工作部分，可補足我的工作部分。（動詞）

- A field trip can be a good complement to our education.
校外考察旅行，對我們教育有補助性。（名詞）

· The various types of gifts are nice complements for your anniversary.
不同禮物，使你的週年紀念更美好。（名詞）

· Her husband complimented her with a new watch on her birthday.
老公為她生日送新錶。（動詞）

· I like to give her a compliment for her good writing.
我誇獎她的寫作。（名詞）

 conscious 與 conscience　　🔊 266

conscious：形容詞，指一個人的神志還是清醒的（having one's mental faculties awake）。反之，失去知覺，或神志不清，就是 unconscious

conscience：名詞，是指一個人良心上的對或錯（moral sense of right or wrong）

例句

· With acupuncture, a patient is supposed to remain conscious during surgery.
使用針灸的過程中，病人應該是清醒的。

· The victim was still conscious after a serious injury in the car accident.
車禍嚴重受傷後，傷者的神志還是清醒的。

· A patient in a vegetative state can stay unconscious for years.
一位植物人，可能多年失去知覺。

· To tell lies all the time can be something against one's conscience.
老是說謊會使一個人良心受到責備。

- For the sake of good conscience, we should not mistreat other people.
  為了良心行事，我們不該虐待他人。

>> convince 與 persuade　　　🔊 267

convince：動詞，「說服」的意思，convince 是著重使人相信（to get someone to believe something）而且後面多半跟子句或帶有介詞的片語

persuade：動詞，「說服」的意思，通常是說服某人去做某事（to get someone to do something），而且後面是跟不定詞

例句

- The police convinced the robber that his situation was hopeless.
  警察使強盜相信他的作犯情況無望。

- She will convince you of his guilt.
  她會使你相信他有罪。

- The police persuaded the robber to drop his gun.
  警察勸服強盜放下槍枝。（後接不定詞 to drop）

>> council 與 counsel　　　🔊 268

council：名詞，是指委員會或代表會，或指一群人為了某事而在一起（a group of people who meet together for something）

counsel：名詞或動詞，意思是協商、討論或給人忠告（to give words of advice）

至於 counselor（或 counsellor）是指顧問或輔導員或律師（the person who gives advice, usually a lawyer）

例句

· The city council will discuss the annual budget next week.
市議會下週將要討論年度預算。

· The ten-member educational council will meet every month.
十人的教育委員會，每月開會一次。

· He has been serving as a council member for special education.
他擔任特殊教育的委員。

· The council refused to listen to her counsel.
委員會不聽她的忠告。（counsel 是名詞）

· If you apply for a job, you better seek counsel from your professor.
假如你申請工作，你最好請教你的教授。（counsel 是名詞）

· The committee counseled me into the late evening.
委員會與我協商到深夜。（counseled 是動詞）

· Every American high school provides guidance counselors for its students.
美國每一所高中都設有學生輔導員。

· Mr. A has served as her personal counselor（或 counsellor）for many years.
A 先生多年來擔任她的私人顧問。

≫ course 與 dish

---

course：指一道一道的菜上桌

---

dish：指許多不同的菜同時排在桌上

例句

· There will be ten dishes of food.
將會有十道菜。（這裡 of food 是需要的，否則也許會誤會為十個空盤子。

· We are having ten dishes for the party.
我們在宴會上準備十盤菜。（在 dish 後面就不必再加 of food）
如果使用動詞 serve，在 dish 或 course 後面不必再加 of food，因為那是必然的。

· They served ten courses.
或 Ten courses were served.
或 We had a ten-course dinner last night.

假如是強調每隔十多分鐘上一道菜，那麼也可以說：
· Ten courses were staggered at 10-15 minutes intervals.
stagger 是動詞，意思是把時間錯開。

· As most Chinese are very hospitable, they will serve many dishes（或 courses）for the guests.
大部分老中很好客，他們為客人準備很多菜。

當然 course 最常用的意思是「課程」和「方向」。

例句

· The student has taken many courses at school.
學生在學校修了很多課程。

· You have taken the wrong course for your future.
你的未來走錯方向了。（course = direction）

》》 date 與 day 🔊 270

----

date：通常指日期

----

day：多半是指星期幾

例句

· What date is today?
今天是幾號？

Today is January 6.
今天是元月六號。

· What day (of the week) is today?
今天是星期幾？

Today is Friday.
今天是星期五。

· I try to keep the information up to date.
我設法保持資料更新。

· The up-to-date issues have been discussed.
當前問題已被討論。
（up-to-date = current，當形容詞用，一般加 hyphen，但無嚴格
規定）

----

date 也指男女約會

例句

· He has a date with his girlfriend.
他和女朋友約會。

⟫ dedicate 與 delicate

dedicate：動詞，意思是獻身、奉獻（名詞是 dedication）

delicate：形容詞，意思是精細的、雅致的或微妙的（名詞是 delicacy）

例句

· Many physicians have been dedicating themselves to finding a cancer cure.
許多醫生獻身於探索一種癌症的治療。

· He always dedicates his weekends to watching sports.
他總是把週末用來看球賽。

· The U.S. considers Taiwan as a delicate political issue.
美國認為台灣是個微妙的政治問題。

· The world economy is still in delicate condition.
世界的經濟情況仍然脆弱。

· This Chinese dish is the delicacy of the season.
這道中菜是應時美味。（多數是 delicacies）

delegate：動詞，指授權；當名詞用是代表成員、代表團團員

例句

· Congress has delegated the emergency power to the President.
國會授予總統緊急應變的權力。

· In recent years, there are many delegates from China to the U.S.
近年來許多中國代表來美國。

➤➤ deliberate 與 deliberately ◀))) 272

---

deliberate：動詞，意思是細心考慮（ think very carefully ）（名詞是 deliberation ）

---

deliberate：形容詞，也有深思的、故意的意思

---

deliberately：副詞，也是故意的意思

例句

· The judge deliberated before he made a final decision.
  法官在做最後決定前經過細心考慮。
  或 After a long deliberation, the decision was made.

· This is a deliberate act of breaking the law.
  這是一個存心破壞法律的行為。
  也就是說：Even though he thought carefully, he still did it on purpose.

· Mr. A made the mistake deliberately.
  A 先生故意犯錯。

· Deliberately, she was trying to defy his authority.
  她故意違抗他的權威。

➤➤ delicate 與 delicacy ◀))) 273

---

delicate：形容詞，意思是優美的，細嫩的，精緻的（ gentle and refined ）。

---

delicacy：名詞，多半指文雅，溫柔，也指佳餚，美味（ refined manners and fine taste ）

例句

- This beautiful lady has delicate skin.
  這位漂亮女人有細嫩的皮膚。

- I have bought a delicate piece of embroidery from China.
  我從中國買來一件精細的刺繡。

- His wife has a certain delicacy.
  她的太太有一種很好的氣質。（ = a person of refined manners）

- Caviar is considered to be a delicacy.
  魚子醬是一道佳餚。（caviar = caviare = fish eggs 法文）

- My friend invited me to a dinner with delicacies of the season.
  我朋友請我一頓山珍海味的美食。

- They offered many table delicacies for the party.
  他們為宴會準備了滿桌的佳餚。

注意，如果說：
- She is in a delicate condition.
  她懷孕了。（delicate condition = pregnant）

desert 與 dessert

🔊 274

desert：名詞，是沙漠 [ˋdɛzɚt]

desert：動詞，是擅離、遺棄 [dɪˋzɝt]

dessert：名詞，是飯後的甜點 [dɪˋzɝt]

例句

- China is a country with many deserts.
  中國有許多沙漠。

- She finally deserted her boyfriend after a two-year relationship.
經過兩年的交往，她最後拋棄了她的男友。

- Americans usually like to have a dessert after dinner.
美國人通常喜歡每餐後吃甜點。

---

deserts：名詞，又有功過、賞罰的意思。

例句

- Many Chinese people failed to get their just deserts.
許多中國人沒有得到公正的賞罰。

---

deserve：動詞，意思是應得，值得

- Mr. Chen deserves a promotion after so many years of good service.
陳先生這麼多年的優良服務，應該得到升級。

❯❯ drunk 與 drunken　　🔊 275

---

drunk：形容詞，都有「酒醉」的意思。drunk 通常是指受到酒的影響（intoxicated），多半放在動詞後面。

---

drunken：形容詞，是指酒醉後的行為（intoxicated behavior）而且一般放在名詞或動詞之前。

例句

- The driver was drunk.
司機酒醉了。（放在動詞 was 之後）

- The man was caught drunk at home.
這男子酒醉在家被捕。（放在動詞 caught 之後）

・The drunken driver caused the accident.
　酒醉的司機造成車禍。（放在名詞 driver 之前）

・Lawmakers try to crack down on drunken driving.
　立法者想要制止酒醉開車。（放在動名詞 driving 之前）
或 Congress has agreed to a tough standard for drunken driving.

如果只說：“He was a drinking driver.” 未必就是酒醉，只是喝些酒而已。

》》 eavesdrop 與 overhear　　　　🔊 276

---

eavesdrop：從屋檐（eaves）而來，就是有意的偷聽或竊聽（動詞時態：eavesdropped, eavesdropping）

---

overhear：無意中從旁聽到或偶然聽到（動詞時態：overheard, overhearing）

例句

・It is impolite to eavesdrop on another's phone conversation.
　竊聽別人的電話是不禮貌的。
　（用介詞 on，是指在電話另一邊偷聽；而用 to 是指不在電話另一邊，只是偷聽別人在說話而已。）

・Some information can be eavesdropped on through electronic equipment.
　有些資料可以由電子設備竊聽而來。（凡是用電子設備竊聽，都用 eavesdrop on）

・I overheard that they were getting divorced.
　我偶然聽到他們要離婚的消息。

· When you stand beside him, you may overhear what he has to say.
你站在他旁邊，就會無意中聽到他要說的話。

ethnic 與 ethical ◀)) 277

ethnic：形容詞，多指種族的，或少數民族的

ethical：形容詞，是指倫理的，道德的

例句

· There are many ethnic groups in the U.S.
在美國有許多不同的種族。

· Can we avoid ethnic conflicts in America?
在美國能防止種族上的衝突嗎？

· As far as ethical conduct is concerned, he is out of line.
從道德規範來說，他是離譜了。

· Is it unethical for physicians to advertise?
醫師登廣告自我宣傳不合乎職業道德嗎？

· Chinese education should stress more on students' ethical conduct rather than just knowledge from a book.
中國教育應該重視學生的道德品格，不是僅僅獲得書本知識。

ex-spouse 與 late spouse ◀)) 278

ex-spouse：spouse 指配偶，前面加 ex，多半指離了婚，也許還活著（generally refer to divorced person; maybe still alive）

late spouse：但是在 spouse 前面加 late，則多半指已故的丈夫或妻子

例句

· Her ex-husband was a warm-hearted person.
他的前夫很熱情。
或 Her ex-husband was warm-hearted.
或 Her ex-husband had a warm heart.
（warm-hearted 指熱情的，而 cold-hearted 是冷淡的）

· His late wife was a high school teacher.
他已逝的太太曾是高中老師。

至於 spouse 前面加 former，也是指離了婚的配偶，也許還活著

例句

· Her former husband has already re-married.
他的前夫已經再婚。
可見 ex-husband（或 wife）與 former husband（或 wife）意義
相同。

》 famous 與 notorious　　　　　　　🔊 279

famous：形容詞，有「著名的」、「眾所周知的」的意思，通常是指好的方面（名詞是 fame）

notorious：指不好的面或有惡名昭彰的味道（名詞是 notoriety）

例句

· There are several notorious persons mentioned in the
headlines of the newspaper.
報上大標題提到幾位劣跡昭彰的人物。

- The man was notorious for robbing banks.
這男子搶銀行出了名。

- Maryland is famous for its blue crabs.
馬里蘭州的藍腳螃蟹很有名（famous = noted = well-known）

- Mr. Wang has been famous for creative writing.
王先生寫創作性的文章很有名氣。

» farther 與 further 🔊 280

farther：形容詞或副詞 far 的比較級，farther一般是指距離
（refer to distance）意思是更遠的，較遠的

further：也是形容詞或副詞 far 的比較級，多半指程度，或進一步
程度（greater degree or extent）

例句

- The location of the meeting I will attend is much farther away.
我要參加的會議地點，是滿遠的。

- Have you walked farther than three miles?
你走了比三哩更遠的路嗎？

- Frankly speaking, I need your further information on (in) this matter.
老實說，這件事我需要進一步的資料。（用介詞 in 表示這件事自己也牽連在內，用 on，就表示自己不牽連在內。

» feces 與 manure 🔊 281

feces（或 faeces）：指「糞便」，是指人的糞便（或用 stool）

manure：多半是指大小動物的糞便（animal waste）諸如 hog, horse, cow, chicken，不過也有老外指寵物狗貓的大便為 feces，因為他們認為 pet 也是家庭的一分子

例句

· Many Americans use horse (cow, chicken) manures in their gardens as fertilizers.
許多美國人在他們菜園裡使用馬、牛、雞糞為肥料。
（一般在美國的 manure 是經過化學處理過）
雖然，中國農夫也在田園裡使用包括沒有化學處理過的人糞為肥料，但在美國則罕見，所以也不用 feces。

· Human feces are chemically treated in order not to pollute the environment.
人糞要經化學處理才不致汙染環境。

· Some patients use laxatives to soften their stools.
有些病人用通便劑使大便變軟。（也有人用 feces，不過醫院裡所說的大便檢查，要用 stool test）

» fire 與 lay-off

◀) 282

fire：動詞，「解雇」因工作不勝任或做錯事等等，將來沒有再被雇用的可能。

lay-off：動詞／名詞，指被解雇是因服務單位財政困難，一旦情況好轉，還有再被雇回的可能。（用過去式 laid 時，多半不用連字符 hyphen）（動詞時態：lay, laid, laid）

例句

· He was fired (because of incompetence).
他被解雇。（一般不說解雇原因，以示禮貌）

- He was laid off.
  他被解雇。

- The company will lay-off 100 workers.
  這家公司將解雇 100 名員工。（這裡 lay-off 是動詞，中間多半加 hyphen）

- There are thousands of lay-offs in the U.S.
  美國有數千名遭解雇的員工。（這裡 lay-off 當名詞用，後面可加 s）

此外，也可以說：

- His position was eliminated.（或 down-sized）
  他的職位被取消了。（指他離職是因服務單位預算減少，所以把他的職位取消了。

可見用 lay-off 或 eliminate 職位，都是表示離職不是自己的錯。而 resign 則是自己辭職：

- He resigned from his job because of health reasons.
  他辭職是因為健康的理由。

» flirt 與 ogle ◀)) 283

---

flirt：動詞，有「送秋波」或「調情」的意味。多指用字眼或言語去挑逗，而且是做不及物動詞，後面多跟介詞 with

---

ogle：動詞，多指做媚眼，或眉來眼去，且是及物動詞，所以後面直接跟受詞。

例句

- Bob has flirted with Susan for hours.
  Bob 對 Susan 挑逗了數個鐘頭。

- They flirt with each other.
  他們彼此擠眉弄眼。

- He stood on the corner flirting with passing girls.
  他站在角落和經過的女子調情。

- He has ogled Lucy for weeks.
  他對 Lucy 調情已經好幾個星期了。

- Will ogling a woman be considered sexual harassment?
  對女性調情算是性騷擾嗎？

---

flirt：名詞，意思是喜歡盯著女人看的男人

例句

- He is a long-time flirt with beautiful girls.
  或者 He has a long flirtation with pretty women.
  他一向愛看漂亮女人。（flirtation 是名詞）

然而男人愛看女人較流行的說法還有：
- He is a heavy girl-watcher.
  或 He likes girl-watching.
  但通常不用 woman-watcher 或 woman-watching）

當然對女人也可以說：
- she is a man-watcher.
  或 She likes man-watching.
  她喜歡看男人。
  （但通常不用 boy-watcher 或 boy-watching）

›› flogging 與 spanking

🔊 284

---

flog：鞭打或棒打，多半有永久性的受傷（permanent injure）
（動詞時態：flogged, flogged, flogging）

---

spank：通常是指用手打（屁股）；是輕微的處分，也不會有永久性的傷害（light form of punishing with hand; no permanent effect）

例句

- The school does not have the authority to flog the student.
  學校無權鞭打處罰學生。

- Back in the old days, they gave the ill-behaved man a flogging.
  過去他們對行為不良的男人，狠狠抽打一頓。

- Many people in America decry flogging as a punishment.
  許多美國人公開譴責以鞭打為處罰。

- Some countries still allow schools to flog the students for disobedience.
  有些國家仍然允許校方對不聽話的學生採取鞭打。

- Many people decry flogging (or caning).
  很多人反對鞭打或棒打。

- The mother gave her boy a spank (or spanking) for being very rude.
  由於孩子的粗魯無禮，他媽媽打他屁股。

- Many parents tend to spank their kids at home.
  許多父母在家有打孩子屁股的傾向。

- Spanking is prohibited at most American schools.
  多數美國學校禁止打學生屁股。

  注意：flog 不可與 frog 弄錯

- She sang with a frog in her throat.
  她帶著沙啞的聲音唱歌。
  （a frog in one's throst 是俚語）

---

cane：動詞，是用手杖打人（是 **flogging** 的一種）（動詞時態是：caned, caning）

例句

- The man was caned by the robber.
  這個人被強盜用手杖打。

》 flyer 與 fryer

🔊 285

---

flyer（或 **flier**）：指只有幾頁供人閱讀的冊子（a pamphlet）或廣告的傳單（advertising circular），有時也指飛行員

---

fryer：指 young chicken，美國人認為可用做美味可口的炸雞（good for deep fry）

例句

- They will be sending out a flyer next week.
  下星期他們要分發一份小冊子。

- Mr. A is a flier for the American Airlines.
  A 先生是美國航空公司的飛行員。

- His wife bought some fryers for the dinner party.
  他老婆買了一些晚宴用的炸雞。

≫ foot 與 feet

◀)) 286

---

foot：腳；呎（單數）

---

feet：腳；呎（複數）

如果用在量度或測量時（measurement），諸如高度或長度，往往容易弄錯。

一般來說，單數 foot，表示呎（= 12 inches）那常放在名詞之前當形容詞用。

例句

· She is a five-foot woman.
　她是五呎高的女人。

· Mr. A is a six-foot three-inch man.
　A 先生是六呎三吋的男人。

　注意：foot 與 inch 都是單數，且用 hyphen
　以上也可用 feet 來表示高度，不過要把 feet 放在名詞後面。

例句

· She is a woman five feet tall.
　（feet 放在名詞 woman 之後，而且 five 和 feet 之間，不加
　　hyphen）

· Mr. A is a man six feet three inches tall.
　（feet 放在名詞 man 之後，inch 也要變成複數，後面再加 tall）

所以：
· This is a ten-foot boat.
= This boat is ten feet long.
或 This boat is ten feet five inches long.
= This is a ten-foot five-inch boat.

同理：

· That is a two-hour show.

= That show is two hours long.

---

foot：當動詞，是付帳的意思（= to pay the bill）

· Hs is footing his bills for tuition, room and board.
他在付學費和膳宿費。

⟫ forbid 與 prohibit

🔊 287 Part 4

---

forbid：動詞，「禁止」的意思，通常後面跟不定詞

---

prohibit：動詞，也是「禁止」之意，後面多半跟名詞與介詞片語

例句

· All state employees are forbidden to strike.
所有州政府人員不准罷工。

· The law prohibits the possession of unlicensed handguns.
法律禁止擁有無照的槍枝。

或

· The law prohibits citizens from possessing unlicensed handguns.

⟫ foul play 與 homicide

🔊 288

---

foul play：指懷疑某種暴行是否有謀殺的可能（suspicious circumstance leads to one's death），後面多半有「死亡」的字眼。

homicide：指已經死亡，但未必是自殺（someone caused a person's death, but may not be self-inflicted or commit suicide），後面不再提「死亡」字眼。

例句

· The police reported that there was a foul play in the death.
警察報導有件暴力致死的案件。（句後有 death 字眼）

· The FBI agents are investigating a homicide case.
聯邦調查局人員正在調查一件謀殺案。（句子後面不再加 death）

---

self-inflicted：指用槍、刀等方式，自我損傷，而且通常後面說明損傷的方式（inflict 是動詞，infliction 是名詞）

例句

· He was killed by a self-inflicted gunshot.
他舉槍自盡。

· The man's sliced wrists were self-inficted.
這男子割腕自殘。
（commit 的動詞時態是：committed, committing）
（slice 當動詞，意為用刀片割）

· He tried to kill himself by using self-inflicted drug overdose.
他想服用過量藥物而尋短見。

›› fruit 與 citrus fruit　　　🔊 289

fruit：指一般性的水果

---

citrus fruit：多半指有厚皮（thick skin）的柑橘類水果，諸如 orange, grape-fruit, citron, lemon 等。

例句

- Fruits and veggies should be served every day.
  每天都該吃水果和蔬菜。（veggies = vegetables）

- Citrus fruits have a lot of Vitamin C.
  柑橘類水果富有維他命 C。

- Generally, citrus fruits are grown in warm areas.
  一般而言，柑橘類水果生長在較熱的地區。

≫ hail from 與 come from　　　　◀) 290

hail from：指出生地或原籍（generally refer to your native place where you were born）

----

come from：指從那裡搬來的

例句

- Where do you hail from?
  你原籍是那裡？（注意：hail 與 hell 發音不同）
你可回答：I hail from China.
  我在中國出生。（注意：通常不用過去式，也就是不用 did 或 hailed）

但如果別人問：
- Where are you from?（不用過去式 were）
= Where do you come from？（不用過去式 did）
= Where did you move from？（不用現在式 do）

就可以答：
- I am from Taiwan.（不用過去式 was）
= I come from Taiwan.（不用過去式 came）

= I moved from Taiwan.（不用現在式 move）

※詢問或回答「出生地」或「從那裡來」，動詞不用過去式，除非表示那個人已經去世。對第二、第三人稱也是如此。

» hard-core 與 soft-core　🔊 291

hard-core：用在色情方面時，係指一絲不掛，赤裸裸的性愛動作（totally naked or explicitly sex act）

soft-core：指一部份的裸體，有時也指全裸（partially naked; sometimes totally naked）

例句

· This is a hard-core（或 soft-core）magazine（或 movie / film）.
這是色情書刊（電影）。
（也就是所謂的 pornography 或 porno）

然而，另一用法是指一個人對信仰十分堅定，是忠誠份子（to be very rigid in one's belief）諸如對政黨忠心耿耿，永遠為自己的政黨而投票。
（always vote for one's political party）

例句

· Mr. A is a hard-core Democrate.
A 先生永遠投民主黨的票，忠誠到底。

假如說：

· Mr. B is a soft-core Republican.
B 先生對共和黨不是那麼忠心耿耿，（雖然他登記共和黨，但投票時，他可能改變主意，投向民主黨。）

- He is a hard-core liberal.
  他堅持自己一定是自由派，絕非保守派。

- Mr. C is a soft-core conservative.
  C 先生不是真正的保守派，有時可能變為自由派。

» healthy 與 healthful　　　◁) 292

healthy：形容詞，指一個人的身體健康，強壯的（refers to one's health）

---

healthful：指對健康有益的食物或有營養價值的（refers to nutrition or foods）

例句

- Vegetables and fruits are supposed to be healthful foods.
  蔬菜和水果是有益健康的食物。
  （也有老外用 healthy）

- Exercising and non-smoking are healthful habits.
  運動和不吸菸是有益健康的習慣。

- This old man looks very healthy.
  這位老人的身體看來很健康。

- In order to keep healthy, you need to eat some seafood.
  為了保持身體健康，你必須吃些海鮮。

» heterosexual 與 bisexual　　　◁) 293

heterosexual：指異性的，也就是男女相愛或性愛

---

bisexual：指兩性的，是指兩性相愛（即愛女人，也愛男人）

例句

· The common sexual orientation should be heterosexual.
一般的性趨向是男女的異性相愛。

· Usually bisexual relationship will be considered abnormal.
一般而言，愛女人，也愛男人是不正常的關係。

---

homosexual：指男人愛男人的同性戀（也叫 gay），而 lesbian 是指女人愛女人的同性戀（但 homosexual 有時也指 lesbian）

---

transgendered：指開過刀的變性人

例句

· He (She) has been considered a transgendered person.
或 His (Her) sexual orientation is transgendered.
他（她）被認為是變性人。

---

transvestite：（拉丁文）意思是異性裝扮癖者（dress like an opposite sex）

例句

· He (She) is a transvestite.
他（她）有異性裝扮癖。

》home 與 house　　　◀) 294

---

house：通常只是指一棟房子或一個 building，可能屋裡是空空的，沒有人住

---

home：多半是指房子裡有人住，有家具，有裝飾，有「家」的溫暖，並且比較 personal

例句

· Home, sweet home!
金窩銀窩，不如自己的草窩。
或 No home is better than your personal home.
或 There's no place like home.

· Make your house into a home.
把你的房子變成一個家。

· The company has built many houses for sale.
公司蓋了許多出售的房子。

· This is my house (home).
這是我的房子（家）。
或 He will sell you a house (home).
他把房子（家）賣給你。
（這是每個人的想法不同而已。）

≫ hook 與 hooker

◀)) 295

hook：名詞，釣鉤，

hooker：名詞，指妓女（= whore）

例句

· Are you taking your fishing hook with you?
你帶了釣魚鉤嗎？

· We hanged up our clothes with hooks.
我們把衣服掛在衣鉤上。
（hooks = coathooks）

- She has been a hooker for many years.
  她當了多年妓女。

或 She hooks her customers.（這裡 hook 當動詞）
  她勾引顧客。（即妓女）

- Being a hooker can be a dangerous profession.
  賣春這行業會很危險的。

》 hot 與 heated   ◀) 296

----

hot：形容詞，指「熱」

----

heated：形容詞，也指「熱」

兩者如果用在「辯論」或「爭吵」時，也有「激烈的」（intense）的意思。

但用 debate 時，通常前面多用 heated；用 argument 時，多半用 hot。

例句

- They had a heated debate at the meeting.
  開會時激烈的辯論。

- The newly-wed had a hot argument last night.
  新婚夫婦昨晚大吵一陣。

----

heat：若當動詞，就是一般的「加熱」

- I have heated this plate of food in the microwave (oven).
  這盤菜在微波爐加熱。（oven 可省略）

- This room is not well heated.
  這房間不暖和。

hot：當形容詞，還可以指天氣炎熱、生氣、脾氣暴躁或指很吃香的行業等，使用時，要看上下文的意思，不能斷章取義。

例句

· It is hot today.
今天天氣很熱。（主詞要用 it）

· The food is hot.
食物很熱。（是指溫度的熱）

如果指放了胡椒等辛辣物時，最好說：
· The food is spicy hot.
這食物很辣。

· He is hot in his field.
他在他的專業領域炙手可熱。（hot = popular）

· When he (she) disagrees with something, he (she) gets hot.
當他不同意一件事，他就生氣。（hot = upset）

---

hot 也可指「性衝動」（sexual arousal）

例句

· When he meets his girlfriend, he gets hot.
他看到他的女友就衝動。

所以不要輕易對女人說：I am hot.，除非馬上補上一句：I sweat all the time. 否則對方也許幽默的回答：

· You may need a cold shower.
你可以沖冷水澡。
（因為沖個冷水浴，可以壓制慾念。）

或

· You may tell your wife.（假如你有太座的話）

>> illegible 與 unreadable

◀)) 297

---

illegible：形容詞，專指字跡不清楚，不易辨認（反義字是 legible）

---

unreadable：形容詞指難讀的，不能讀的，或讀起來枯燥無味。多指在文字上喜歡用難字或咬文嚼字。

例句

· My friend Andy's handwriting is illegible.
  我朋友 Andy 寫的字很難辨認。

· The ink has faded so much that many words are illegible.
  墨水顏色褪了，以致許多字看不清楚。

· I have found this article virtually unreadable.
  我發覺這篇文章很難讀。

反之 readable 就是易讀的，讀起來有趣味或可讀性強的。

· His articles are very readable and helpful.
  他的文章可讀性強且有用。

>> immigrant 與 emigrant

◀)) 298

Immigrant：移民（動詞是 immigrate，名詞是 immigration）係指由其他國家遷移到本國來的人。

---

emigrant（動詞是 emigrate，名詞是 emigration），指由本國遷移到其他國家的人。

以美國人立場，來自台灣的華人，就是他們的 immigrant，而到台灣居住的美國人，以美國人立場，又是 emigrant 了。同理，站在

台灣人民立場來說，在台居住的美國人，就是 immigrant，由台灣遷到美國的華人，又是 emigrant 了。

例句

· We have more immigrants than emigrants in the U.S.
  在美國進來的移民，要比出去的移民多。

· There are many emigrants from the U.S. living in Taiwan.
  住在台灣的美國僑民也很多。

▶▶ incident 與 accident

◀) 299

incident：名詞，「意外事情」或「偶發事件」，多半是指伴隨而來的事故、小插曲，通常是較小的意外事情

accident：「意外事情」，是指一件突然發生的不幸意外，或事先無法控制的意外遭遇或不測事件

例句

· There was a serious auto accident yesterday.
  昨天有件嚴重的車禍。（突然發生，事先無法控制）

· This is an industrial accident because an employee has been injured by the machine.
  這是一件工業意外事故，因為一位員工被機器弄傷。

· The strikers have caused the company many incidents.
  罷工者已造成公司許多意外的事情。（人事方面的麻煩等等）

當形容詞和副詞等，意義也大致相同。
· The rate of accidental death has increased since last year.
  去年以來意外事故死亡率增加了。

233

- There was an incidental meeting of two leaders between Cuba and the U.S.
  古美兩國的領導人偶然碰面。

- Accidentally, the child was hit by a motor bike.
  不料,孩子被機車撞上。

- Incidentally, I met an old friend on the street.
  無意中,我在路上遇到老友。

» inflammable 與 inflammatory　　◀》 300

inflammable:形容詞,指易燃的,性情暴躁的(動詞是 inflame; 名詞是 inflammation)

inflammatory:形容詞,指煽動性的,意圖使人激憤的

例句

- Never put any inflammable substances near a fire.
  不可在火旁放置易燃物品。

- No one would like to deal with inflammable person.
  沒有人喜歡跟脾氣暴躁的人交往。

- Some politicians love to give inflammatory speeches.
  一些政客喜歡作煽動性的講演。

- He will not write any inflammatory articles for the newspaper.
  他不為報紙寫帶有刺激煽動性的文章。

» inhabit 與 inhibit　　◀》 301

inhabit:意思是居住,棲息(多半指動物)

inhibit：禁止、阻止的意思

_例句_

· Birds generally inhabit wooded areas.
鳥通常棲息在樹林地區。（inhabit 在這裡是及物動詞）

· Her boss inhibits her from getting a sideline job.
她的老闆阻止她另找副業。

· Miss Wang's strict upbringing has inhibited her from asking questions.
王小姐的嚴格教養使她怯於發問。

》 lemon 與 lime　　　　🔊 302

lemon：一般指黃皮的檸檬

lime：指綠皮的檸檬。

品質差的貨品，也叫 lemon（但不叫 lime）

_例句_

· I prefer lemon juice rather than orange juice.
我喜歡檸檬汁而不喜歡橘子汁。

· The seemingly good car turned out to be a lemon.
看來似乎是好車，結果是爛貨。

· The brand new tires have proved to be lemons.
全新的車胎證實是差勁的貨。

>> let 與 leave

🔊 303

let：意思是許可，或允許（to allow or to permit）（動詞時態是：let, let, let, letting）

leave：指從某個地方離開，或把某件事留下後再走開（to go away from or to place something and then go away），也表示「不要改變」或「不要干擾」（not to change or disturb）（動詞時態是：leave, left, left, leaving）

例句

· Don't let your dog roam free.
　不要讓你的狗隨便到處走。（let = allow）

· Will you let your daughter go with him to the party?
　你讓你的女兒和他參加宴會嗎？（let = allow or permit）

· I let him leave if he has done his work.
　假如他做完工作，我就讓他走。（let = permit ; leave = go away）

· You may leave your book on my desk.
= Place your book and go away from it.
　你可把你的書留在我的書桌上。

· Please leave the door open.
　請不要關門。（= Don't close it.）

· Leave Mary alone when she is sad.
　當 Mary 難過時，別去打擾她。（= Don't disturb her.）

· After the meeting many students have left.
　開會後，許多學生離開了。（= have departed）

· The boy has been left at the shopping center.
　這男孩被遺留在購物中心。

≫ lightning 與 lightening

lightning：名詞，指閃電

lightening：意思是減輕重量或負擔（to make it lighter in weight or burden）（動詞是 lighten）

例句

· Lightning will come with a thunder storm.
閃電與暴風雨同時來臨。

或 Lightening comes before thunder.
暴風雨前有閃電。

· The lightening of the load is the only solution to save the ship.
減輕載重是唯一救船的辦法。

· The lightening of schoolwork will be helpful to the secondary students.
減少學校功課負擔對中學生有幫助。

lighting 又指燈光的照明

例句

· The bright lighting of this house drew the attention of many passers-by.
這房子的明亮燈光引起許多路人的注意。（passer-by 是單數）

· Christmas lights are lighting up the town.
聖誕節的燈光照亮了城市。

loose 與 lose

◀)) 305

loose：形容詞，意思是寬鬆的、沒紮緊（not securely attached; not tight enough）

lose：動詞，意思是失去（to suffer loss）（動詞時態是：lose, lost, lost, losing）

例句

· The screw on the machine seems loose; you need to tighten it up.
這機器的螺絲釘鬆了，你要上緊。

· If the door lock is loose, it will not serve the purpose.
如果門鎖鬆了，那就鎖不住，沒有用。

· Many Chinese still use loose-leaf tea rather than tea bags.
許多老中還用散裝茶葉，而不用茶袋。

· Be aware; Mr. Lee often has a loose tongue.
要知道，李先生常常信口亂說。

· I am sure she is not a loose girl.
我相信她不是一位放蕩女孩。

· When you go shopping, don't lose your child in the crowd.
你去採購時別在人群中丟了小孩。

· Many young Americans have lost their lives in the war.
許多年輕美國人在戰爭中失去生命。

表示遺失或損失，也可用名詞 loss：

· Mr. Lee's first year of business ended in a loss.
李先生第一年的生意虧本了。

· Your resignation will be a great loss to our company.
你的辭職對我們公司將是一大損失。

» love 與 lover

🔊 306

love：一般指 emotional 的愛，也就是 someone cares about you，不過老外也把 love 當做男女的情人

lover：多半是指有性關係的情人，或是同居（live-in）的男女朋友或是 mistress（情婦）

例句

· He (She) is my love.
（未必有性關係）

或者只說：He (She) is the one I love.

當你介紹「另一半」給老外時，如果說：「他（她）是我的愛人。」He(She)is my lover. 老外也許以為只是姘居的情人。如果你一定要用 lover 這個字，那麼為了避免誤會，也可以說：She (He) is my lover and my wife (husband).

» low-key 與 low-profile

🔊 307

low-key：形容詞，是指有意地採取低姿態，低調的，節制的或不太重視

low-profile：形容詞，多指一個人的性格，不愛拋頭露面而保持一種低姿態

例句

· The U.S. sometimes takes a low-key approach to (on) the China issue.
美國有時對中國問題採取低姿態。

· Mr. Chang is supposed to be a low-key negotiator.
張先生被認為是克制的談判者。

· He always likes to keep a low-profile.
他喜歡保持一種低姿態，不願常見到別人。（這裡 low-profile 當名詞用）

· Our new director will organize a department of low-profile staff.
我們的新主任，要組織一個不愛出鋒頭的部門。

也可以說：

· This is a high-profile job.
這是常常上報「知名度」高的工作。（但沒有 high-key 的說法）

》 malicious 與 meticulous　　　　🔊 308

---

malicious：意思是刻薄的，惡意的（mean, not kind-hearted）
（名詞是 malice）

---

meticulous：指非常注意細節（neat & very detailed）
這兩個字都是形容詞，拼法相近，容易弄錯。

例句

· This man has been malicious to his co-workers.
這男子對他的同事很刻薄。

· It seemed the charges were false and malicious and particularly injured his reputation.
似乎控告是虛假而險惡的，尤其損害他的名聲。

· She was meticulous with arranging the papers.
她很細心地整理文件。

· The meticulous person often spends too much time on a task.
過分細心的人，對一件事花費太多時間。

memento 與 souvenir ◀》309

memento：名詞，紀念品或引起回憶的東西，比較有 personal 的
意味，且有 memory 的價值

souvenir：名詞，指一般的紀念品，或只是讓你回憶曾經去過什麼
地方（remind you where you went）

例句

· My parents have left many mementos (mementoes) after their
death.
我父母去世後留下許多令人回憶的紀念品。（比較 personal）

· I brought back some mementos after my trip to Taiwan.
我從台灣旅遊帶回一些紀念品。（因為台灣親人多，所以紀念品也
較 personal）

· There are many souvenirs in the gift shop.
在禮品店裡有許多紀念品。

· Susan bought several souvenirs during her visit to China.
蘇姍到中國旅遊時買了一些紀念品。

momentary 與 momentous ◀》310

momentary：形容詞，指片刻的，短暫的（名詞是 moment）

momentous：形容詞，重要的，有影響的

例句

· At hearing the news, Mr. A had a momentary pause.
A 先生聽到消息時，停頓了片刻。

· He has a momentary fear whenever he gives a speech.
他只要演講，都會有點短暫的恐懼。

· It is a momentous decision; you have to think it over very carefully.
這是一種極重要的決定，你要仔細考慮。

---

momentum：名詞，意思是勢頭或衝力（複數是 momentums 或 momenta）

· The young business man is trying to keep the momentum going.
年輕的商人盡力保持發展的勢頭。

· The new style will prevail and pick up momentum.
這新的式樣將會流行而且會有好的勢頭。

» non-smoker 與 smokeless　　◄))） 311

---

non-smoker：名詞，意思是指吸菸者，但現在不吸了（currently does not smoke），多半是指人（refer to people）

---

smokeless：形容詞，指咀嚼菸葉或菸草，而不是吸菸（use tobacco to chew instead of cigarette），也就是不需要點火，也不冒煙（does not need to light it; no smoke comes out）

例句

· This section of the restaurant is for non-smokers.
餐館這個區域是給非吸菸者使用的。

· If you want to be in good health, be a non-smoker.
假如你要健康，就不要吸菸。

· Smokeless tobacco is also prohibited in public.
在公共場所咀嚼菸草，也是禁止的。

· Smokeless tobacco may cause oral cancer.
咀嚼菸草，可能導致口腔癌。

· This store is smokeless.
這個商店，是無菸的。（= no smoke）

· A smokeless environment will be healthful.
無菸的環境，對人們較健康。（=lacking smoke）

» older 與 elder

🔊 312

older；形容詞的比較級，可以指人，也可指物

elder：也是形容詞，意思是年紀較大的，只能指人

例句

· His uncle is older than mine / my uncle.
他的叔叔比我的叔叔老。

· My car is older than his (car).
我的汽車比他的舊。

· Mr. Wang is an elder statesman.
王先生是位老政治家。（元老）

elderly 也可做為形容詞：

· She is an elderly lady.
她是位老太太。

- These elderly people can talk your ears off.
  這些老人會對你喋喋不休，說個不停。

- They are both elderly and set in their ways.
  他們兩位都是長者，並且有他們固定的生活方式。

在 elderly 前加 the，又可指一般的許多老人

例句

- The elderly deserve our respect.
  老人值得咱們的尊敬。

有時 elder 也當名詞用：
- We should assist our elders in all possible ways.
  我們應盡力幫助老人。

至於 younger 也不指物，只能指人：
- She is younger than he (is).

- Your house is newer than mine.
  （不用 younger）

此外，名詞 youngster，則是指一般年輕人：
- He is an outstanding youngster.
  他是位傑出的年輕人。

- Many youngsters have lots of energy.
  許多年輕人富有精力。

註：很少人用 oldster，但老外開玩笑時也用。

» oligopoly 與 monopoly

◀)) 313

oligopoly：名詞，壟斷的意思，指由少數人壟斷某一商場上的買賣

monopoly：通常是指由政府給予的壟斷專賣權

例句

· Is oligopoly in business considered a drawback to capitalism?
少數人壟斷商業買賣是資本主義的缺點嗎？

· Our Energy Department has to deal with an oligopoly of the oil supply.
我們能源部必須處理石油供應的壟斷問題。

· A special plan has been made for monopolies on wine and tobacco.
一個特別的菸酒專賣計畫，已經制訂出來。

至於 oligarchy，是指由少數人控制的寡頭政治。
例句

· Many countries have adopted oligarchy.
許多國家採用寡頭政治。

》 oversee 與 overlook ◀⏹ 314

oversee：動詞，指監督、監視（supervise）

overlook：動詞，指失察、漠視（neglect）

例句

· Mr. Chen oversaw this project.
陳先生監督這個計畫。（動詞時態：oversee，oversaw；overseen）

· The boss overlooked his employee's inappropriate behavior.
上司忽視了他員工不合宜的行為。

peel 與 shell 🔊 315

peel：指將有皮的水果（如：蘋果、橘子、香蕉等）剝皮、去皮

shell：將有硬殼或有莢的食物（如：豆子、花生、核桃等）去殼

shuck：對蠔、蛤蜊去殼

pick：挑螃蟹肉

shear：剪羊毛

pluck：拔雞毛

例句

· He taught kids how to peel an apple.
他教孩子怎麼削蘋果皮。

· She shells peas, beans, peanuts and walnuts.
她把豆子、花生、核桃的殼去掉。

· The man shucks oyster (clam) for sale.
這位男子將蠔去殼來賣。

· He picked one can of crab meat for me.
他剔了一罐蟹肉給我。

· The farmer shears the wool from sheep.
農夫剪羊毛。

· The old man plucked the feather from the chicken.
老翁拔雞毛。

---

personal：形容詞，意思是個人的，私人的（individual）

---

personnel：名詞，意思是人事，指同一單位服務的一群人的總稱
（a group of people working in the same organization）

例句

- At the meeting Mr. Wang gave his personal opinion.
  開會時，王先生表達他個人的意見。

- Most Americans consider it bad manners to ask personal questions.
  美國人多半認為問人家私事是不禮貌的。

- An emphasis on personal hygiene should be stressed in everyday life.
  每天生活中，應該著重個人衛生。

- The personnel of our school range in age from 25 to 75.
  我們學校員工年齡，從 25 歲到 75 歲。
  （如指員工為整體，動詞用 ranges；如指不同年齡員工為個體，則用動詞 range）

- Mrs. A, our personnel director, has been working here for ten years.
  我們人事處主任 A 太太，在此工作已 10 年。

- All personnel of / at this company have been asked to donate money for charity.
  公司請所有同仁為慈善而捐款。
  （如指整體，也可用動詞單數 has）

posture 與 gesture　◀» 317

posture：指坐或立，說話或演講的姿勢或姿態（how you physically stand or sit）

gesture：指說話或打招呼時的手勢（to use hands to express the emotion）

例句

· Your posture behind / by the podium looked very distinguished.
你站在講台後的姿勢顯得很神氣。
（by the podium 是站在講台旁邊）

· A woman's siting posture should be refined and graceful.
女人的坐姿應該文雅而優美。

· Miss Li always enjoys posturing before an audience.
李小姐總喜歡在觀眾面前裝腔作勢。

· Do not use too much gesturing.
或 Do not use too much gestures in your conversation.
說話時不要做太多的手勢。

· A poor gesture in talking is to point at others (with one's fingers).
說話不良的手勢是用指頭指著別人。（with one's fingers 可省）
（**注意**：audience 是集合名詞，雖然意義是多數，但後面不加 s。

>> recreation center 與 entertainment center　◀» 318

recreation center：通常指在一個建築物裡有供大眾進行體能活動（physical activities）的娛樂活動中心（a building where people go to play or exercise）

entertainment center：指在家庭裡放置唱機、電視機或 VCR 等所用的架子，只是一種家具而已（shelving space for entertaining machines such as TV, radio, etc. It's a piece of furniture.）

例句

・The YMCA is an excellent recreation center for our youngsters.
基督教青年會是年輕人很好的娛樂場所。
（YMCA = Young Men's Christian Association）

・In a big city, there are several recreation centers.
在大城市裡都有幾個娛樂中心。

・I bought an entertainment center for my family room.
我為交誼間裡購入了遊樂器。
（family room 是指平時家人看電視，聽唱機等歡聚的房間。）

註：有時美國人也把 mall 裡供孩子玩樂的電動玩具等，叫做 entertainment center。

例句

・The mall functions as an entertainment center.
購中心也有娛樂場所的功能。
（這裡 function 當動詞用）
recreation room 則是指家庭裡供孩子娛樂或親友交誼的房間。

» respectable 與 respectful

◀》 319

respectable：形容詞，「可敬」的意思，特別表示品格高尚等原因，而值得尊敬的（deserving respect）

respectful：「可敬」的意思，指為了禮貌起見而對他人敬重（showing respect）

例句

· His motives (intentions) are respectable.
他的動機是值得尊敬的。

· Be respectful to the elders!
對老年人應該尊敬。

---

respective：也是形容詞，但意思是「各自的」（individual）

例句

· All of us have our respective duties.
我們大家都有各自的義務。

· The service awards were respectively given to the recipients.
服務獎由得獎人分別接受。（加 ly 當副詞用）

---

respecting：介系詞，意思是「關於」、「有關」（= regarding = concerning）

例句

· Respecting this matter, you have to make up your mind.
關於這件事，你必須下定決心。

≫ responsible 與 accountable　　🔊 320

---

responsible：「負責」的意思，但是指範圍較為確定，且較直接的負責（direct responsibility）

---

accountable：「負責」的意思，係指範圍較廣，也較間接的負責（indirect responsibility）

兩者後面的介詞都用 for。

例句

・The comptroller is responsible for the college budget, but the president of the college is accountable for the deficit.
大學主計長是負責預算，但大學校長是負責赤字。

・Mr. Clinton has more responsibilities than his cabinet members.
柯林頓先生比他的閣員有更多的責任。

>> rooster 與 roster ◀》 321

rooster：本是公雞（cock）或雄雞（male chicken），通常指男人

roster：指一群的男人或 a list of people（有時也指軍人的名冊）
（注意：rooster [`rustɚ ] 與 roster [ `rɑstɚ] 發音不同）

例句

・Mr. A is the only rooster in the hen house.
A 先生是女人群中唯一的男人。（即紅中一點綠）
（rooster 指男人，hen 本是母雞，這裡指女人。）

・This person has been added to the roster.
這個人被加入男子名冊裡。

・The teacher prepared a roster of his students.
老師準備一份學生名冊。

・The lawyer made a roster of his clients.
律師為當事人造了名單。

・Her mother told her to get another rooster on the roster.
她媽媽告訴她從一群男人中，選擇另一位男人。

›› shag 與 fuzz　◀)) 322

shag：名詞，通常指粗毛或長毛（形容詞是 shaggy）

fuzz：名詞，指細毛、絨毛或茸毛（形容詞是 fuzzy）

例句

· The shag carpet is out of style.
　粗毛的地毯已經不流行了。

· How much carpet fuzz do you expect to come out？
　你想地毯會起多少的細毛呢？

至於形容詞 shaggy，也指有很多毛的動物，有時也指人。

例句

· The dog / cat is so shaggy.
　狗貓有多長毛。（long hair）

· The man looks very shaggy.
　這位男子長髮、長鬍子，一身毛。
　（不禮貌，不可當面說。）

· Your sweater is fuzzy.
　你的毛衣起了毛球。

›› snob 與 snub　◀)) 323

snob：名詞，指自命不凡或神氣巴拉的人

snub：多半當動詞，意思是冷落或冷漠（動詞時態是：snubbed, snubbing）

例句

- There are many academic snobs in our Chinese community.
  在我們中國人的圈子裡，有許多自命不凡，自封為學者的人。

- He is a snob; nobody really likes to associate with him.
  他是一位自命不凡的人；沒有人喜歡與他來往。

- Mr. Chen was snubbed by his girlfriend.
  陳先生被他的女友冷落。

- The woman snubs him by refusing to see him.
  這女士藉著不見面而冷落他。

» snow job 與 snowball　　🔊 324

snow job：通常當名詞，是指隱瞞某件事情（to cover up something）或以小小事實，誇大其詞（to exaggerate something based on little fact or truth）

snowball：多半當動詞，是指一件事逐漸往不好的方面擴大或增加，就像滾雪球那樣，越滾越大（things built up in a certain negative direction）

例句

- Mr. A did a snow job.
  A 先生想隱瞞某件事情。（= He tried to cover up something.）

- When he came home late, he decided to give his wife a snow job.
  當他回家晚了，他就向太太編造故事。（to make up a story）

- In order to secure the new position, Mr. A tried to give me a snow job.
  為了取得新職位，A 先生誇大其詞，想瞞騙我。

- This problem snowballs every day.
  這個問題每天越搞越大。

- If you continue to lie to your boss, things will snowball.
  假如你繼續對老闆說謊，事情將會愈鬧愈大。

- Nip the problem in the bud before it snowballs.
  在問題擴大之前，應該儘早解決。

---

snowball 當名詞用時，也指真正的雪球。

例句

- The boy threw a snowball at his friend.
  小男孩向他朋友擲雪球。

但如果說：
- He does not have the chance of a snowball in hell.
  他毫無機會。（= He has no chance at all.）

❯❯ soap opera 與 sitcom ◀) 325

---

soap opera：在 TV 上播出的連續劇（serial）或連續性的故事情節，可連續數年，好像沒完沒了

---

sitcom：只是在 TV 上的一種喜劇，通常每次都有不同的主題（an individual story and supposed to be comical）（sit 就是指 situation; com 是指 comedy）

例句

- Soap operas are serials on TV.
  肥皂劇就是電視上的連續劇。

- Sitcoms are supposed to be comical.
  Sitcoms 應該是喜劇。

那麼在美國哪些是屬於 soap opera，那些屬於 sitcom 呢？

舉例來說：
· "General Hospital" is a popular soap opera.
· "The Guilding Light" is a long-running soap opera.
· "Young & Restless" is another soap opera.
· "Everybody loves Raymond"is a popular sitcom on CBS.
· "I love Lucy" show was an original sitcom.

》 sob 與 sober

◀))) 326

---

sob：動詞，意思是哭或感傷（動詞時態：sobbed, sobbed, sobbing）

---

sober：是形容詞，意思是清醒的，也就是知道控制自己行為，雖然喝酒，也不會喝醉。

例句

· She sobbed at her husband's funeral.
  她在亡夫喪禮中十分感傷。

· I tried to comfort her when she was sobbing.
  當她哭泣時，我安慰她。

· To make Mr. A sober from being an alcoholic is nearly impossible.
  要使 A 先生有節制不過量飲酒是近乎不可能。
或 Keeping Mr. A sober is not an easy task.

sometime 與 sometimes

🔊 327

sometime：副詞，指日後，或將來某個時候（at some time in the future）

sometimes：副詞，指有時候（now and then）

例句

· May I come to see you sometime?
那天我能來看你嗎？

· I hope sometime my English can be greatly improved.
盼望有一天我的英語能大大的進步。

· Some people predict that sometime in the future we will not produce enough food.
有人預料有一天我們沒有足夠的食物。

· All machines, no matter how well made, sometimes need repairs.
所有機器，不管多好，有時都要修理。

· His girlfriend is sometimes hot and sometimes cold to him.
他的女友對他時熱時冷。

如果把 some time 分開，有時也指一段時間（a period of time）

例句

· Most new Chinese immigrants in the U.S. need some time to get adjusted.
許多新來美國移民的中國人，需要一段時間才能適應。

⟫ spay 與 sterilize

◀)) 328

spay（或 neuter）：指把動物中性化，不過嚴格來說，spay（或 spaying）多半用在 female animal（即切除卵巢），而 neuter （或 neutering）是用在 male animal

sterilize：指男女做絕育的手術而破壞生殖力

例句

· Dog owners should have their pets spayed or neutered so that unwanted puppies would not face a cruel end.
狗主人該把他們的寵物結紮，以免將來小狗遭遇殘酷命運。

· I feel dogs and cats have to be spayed or neutered.
我認為狗貓都該結紮。

· Having had three children, his wife decided to be sterilized.
有了三個孩子之後，他太太決定結紮。

· He has decided to have a vasectomy (in order to become sterilized).
他決定接受手術切除輸精管。

※一些美國男人希望 vasectomy 後，將來還可再動手術，俾能恢復生育能力，所以他們不願輕易直說：I want to be sterilized. 所以上句中 in order to become sterilized 也可省去。

此外，sterilize 也有「消毒」的意思。

例句

· Hospitals need to sterilize many surgical instruments every day.
醫院每天要消毒許多外科手術器材。

》 standoff 與 stand off　　🔊 329

standoff（或 stand-off）：指造成僵局，或雙方僵持不下（to defy authority or confrontation; neither side wins）

stand off：表示不要被捲入（remove; not to be involved）

例句

· The standoff began after a gun battle with the police.
與警方槍戰之後，雙方僵持不下。

· Taiwan's presidential election in 1996 sparked a tense standoff between the U.S. and China.
1996 年台灣總統選舉造成中美的僵局。
或 Taiwan's stand-off with China remains acrimonious.
台灣與中國大陸的僵持不下，仍然是很劇烈的。（acrimony 是名詞）

· We should stand off from that situation.
我們應該避免那種情況。（stand off = stay away or keep distance）

· The ship stood off from the shore.
船隻遠離岸邊。

但 He is very stand offish.
他很冷淡不友好。
（stand offish = stay away from people）

》 stationary 與 stationery　　🔊 330

stationary：形容詞，意思是固定的，穩定的或不可移動的（in a fixed position or stay in one place）

stationery：名詞，指信紙、信封等文具（materials for writing or writing paper）

例句

· The patient's condition has remained stationary after surgery.
手術後，病人的情況穩定。（= stable）

· The tables in the conference room are stationary.
會議室的桌子是固定的。（= can not be moved around）

· I will need a box of stationery soon.
我將快需要一盒信封信紙。（多指配套的）

· Employees are not supposed to use official stationery for personal purposes.
員工不該用公家文具，當私人用途。

›› surly 與 surely

◀》 331

surly：形容詞，意思是粗魯的，敵意的

surely：副詞，意思是確實地，無疑地

例句

· He is shouting and giving a surly speech.
他大聲地發表有敵意的演說。

· Many salespersons at Chinese stores are often surly to other Chinese.
許多中國商店的營業員，對其他華人的態度很差。

· Surely she is more beautiful than her female friends.
她確實比她的朋友們漂亮些。

· He must surely have known her for many years.
他想必認識她多年了。
（surely 也可放在句首，意思還比放在句中肯定些。）

》 ticket 與 citation　　　　　　◀)) 332

- -

ticket：指入場券（票）外，還指違反交通規則的罰單或違章的通知或傳票

- -

citation：除指嘉獎、表彰外，也指法律上的傳票或傳訊

例句

· He got a speeding citation.（不用 speedy）
他拿到一張開車超速的罰單。（citation = ticket）

· This juvenile will receive a citation for illegal alcohol consumption.
這位少年將收到一張違法喝酒的罰單。
以上兩句所以用 citation 的原因，也許因為當事人不服氣時，可向法庭申訴。

但是如果說：

· Mr. Chen won a citation for an outstanding service.
陳先生獲得優良服務獎。（citation = award）

· His supervisor presented a written citation for his exceptional performance.
他的上司授給他一張工作嘉獎函。（citation = letter of appreciation）

⟫ vocation 與 vacation　　　◀》 333

vocation：指職業或職責

vacation：指度假。

例句

· What type of vocation are you going to take up after your graduation?
你畢業後要找什麼工作？（take up = follow）

· Being a husband and father seems to be one of the vocations of a married man.
當老公和老爸似乎是婚後男人的職責之一。

· The old couple are planning to take a vacation in / to China.
這對老夫婦想到中國度假。（用 in 表示人在中國；用 to 表示人不在中國。

avocation：則指個人的副業或業餘的愛好

· Does he have an avocation on / for the weekends?
他週末有業餘愛好嗎？（用 on 或 for 均可）

⟫ welfare 與 farewell　　　◀》 334

welfare：名詞，是福利、安康的意思

farewell：歡送、離別的意思

例句

· The American government is doing very well on social welfare.
美國政府在社會福利方面做得不錯。

- Chinese officials should not neglect the welfare of the workers.
  中國官員不可忽視工人的福利。

- Our department will have a farewell party for Mr. A.
  我們系裡將為 A 先生舉行一次歡送會。

- We all waved (our last) farewell to the retired director.
  我們向退休的主任揮手告別。

›› wilful 與 stubborn　　🔊 335

wilful（= willful）多半指故意的或存心的固執或不肯做。
（purposely will not do something）而 stubborn 係指天生倔強
的個性，或由後天環境的影響而養成的頑固（will not change one's
mind naturely or nurturely）

例句

- This wilful teenager refused to listen to his parents.
  這位小伙子故意不聽父母的話。

- His secretary was fired because of wilful disobedience.
  他的秘書因存心違抗而被解雇。

- The stubborn man always makes troubles.
  頑固個性的人常惹麻煩。

- He has accomplished this project with stubborn efforts.
  他以頑強的努力完成這項計畫。

›› worthless 與 priceless　　🔊 336

worthless：形容詞，意思是不值錢的，沒有用處的（no price at
all）

priceless：形容詞，指無法標價的，非常昂貴的（have value beyond prices; great value you cannot put prices）

例句

· This lawn-mower has become worthless.
這部鋤草機已經一文不值了。

· Many items at the yardsale are worthless.
在庭院出售舊貨中，有許多東西是不值錢的。

· The pictures of my children at an early age are now priceless to me.
我孩子的童年照片，對我是很貴重的。

· This painting by Picasso is priceless.
這幅畢卡索的畫非常值錢。

money 與 monies　　🔊 337

money：單數是指一般性的貨幣或金錢（general term）

monies（或 **moneys**）：是指來自各方的金錢（money from all different sources）（monies 較常用）

例句

· His father has made lots of money.
他爸爸賺了很多錢。（lots of = a lot of）（一般性的錢）

· Sometimes money is the root of evil.
有時錢是禍害的根源。

· The monies for our new science building came from people in all walks of life.
新科學大樓的經費是來自不同行業的人。
（all walks of life 是指各個行業）

· The charitable organization collected many monies from various sources.
慈善機關的經費是從不同地方收集而來。

❯❯ navy 與 navies　　　🔊 338

navy：單數名詞，指一般性的海軍（general term）

navies：複數是指各國的海軍（navy from different countries）

例句

· The U.S. Navy is very strong.
美國海軍很強大。（單指美國的海軍）

· The navies from different nations will patrol the Persian Gulf.
不同國家的海軍將巡邏波斯灣。

· The British and American navies fight together against terrorism.
英美兩國的海軍為對抗恐怖主義而共同作戰。

· The navies for naval exercises in the Pacific Ocean are from several countries.
太平洋的海軍演習，是由幾個國家組成。

❯❯ fish 與 fishes　　　🔊 339

fish：單數型的是魚的一般通稱

fishes：複數是指魚的不同種類。

例句

- I have caught a lot of fish.
  我抓到很多魚。（是指不分種類的魚）
  （這裡的 fish，也是 collective noun）

- My friend, David, caught many fishes yesterday.
  我朋友 David 昨天捕到很多種類的魚。

» mortgager 與 mortgagee　　　🔊 340

mortgage：指房屋等貸款（名詞或動詞）

---

mortgager：指貸款的機關，如銀行（名詞）

---

mortgagee：指貸款人（名詞）

例句

- The mortgager is where mortgagees obtain their mortgages.
  貸款機關就是貸款者獲得貸款的地方。

- The bank has mortgaged millions of dollars to its mortgagees.
  銀行貸款好幾百萬給貸款者。（mortgage 當動詞用）

其他還有類似用法得字眼

» interviewer 與 interviewee　　　🔊 341

interview：動詞／名詞，「面試」或「會見」

---

interviewer：名詞，「面試者」或「接見者」

---

interviewee：名詞，「被面試的人」或被「接見者」

例句

· The interview was conducted by the interviewer for the interviewee.
面試是面試者為被面試者而舉行的。

≫ donor 與 donee
≫) 342

donate：動詞

donation：名詞

donor：名詞，拉丁文，意思是「贈送人」或「捐款者」= donator

donee：名詞，拉丁文，意思是「得款者」或「接受捐贈者」= donatee 它們也是從 donate 演變而來。

例句

· The donor will give ten thousand dollars to the donee.
捐款人捐贈了一萬元給受捐贈者。

≫ addresser 與 addressee
≫) 343

address：指「地址」

addresser：指「寄信人」或「發信人」

addressee：指「收信人」

例句

· Postage normally will be paid by the addresser instead of the addressee.
郵費通常是由寄信人付的，而不是收信人付的。

›› inviter 與 invitee ◄)) 344

invite：動詞，意思是「邀請」

inviter：名詞，「邀請者」或「主人」

invitee：名詞，「被邀請者」或「客人」

例句

・The inviter will pay the dinner bill for the invitee.
主人將為客人付帳。

›› employer 與 employee ◄)) 345

employ：動詞，「僱用」

employer：名詞，「僱主」或「老闆」，也指「公司」或「機關」

employee：名詞，「受僱者」或「僱員」。

例句

・The employer should hire its employees based on equal
opportunity.
老闆僱用員工應該基於平等機會。

›› biographer 與 biographee ◄)) 346

biograph：動詞「為……寫傳記」= biographize

biography：名詞，「傳記」

biographer：名詞，傳記作者

biographee：傳記的主人公，也是被寫傳記的人或對象。

例句

· The biographer wrote a book about the biographee.
傳記作者寫了一本有關傳記主人公的書。

❯❯ honorer 與 honoree 🔊 347

honor 或 honour：「榮譽」

honorer：指授予榮譽學位的學校或機關

honoree：指接受榮譽學位者，或受獎者

例句

· The honorer presented the honorary degree to the honoree.
學校頒發榮譽學位給受獎者。

❯❯ divorce 與 divorcee 🔊 348

divorce：名詞，指一般的「離婚」

divorce：法文，係指離了婚的男人，兩者發音不同。

divorcee：也是法文，係指離了婚的女人。
不過沒有 divorcer 這個字。

例句

· They both got a divorce; so she is a divorcee and he is a divorce.
他們離婚了，所以她是離了婚的女人，他是離了婚的男人。

· As a divorcee, her self-esteem hit an all-time low.
作為一位離過婚的女人，她的自信心十分低落。

» attender 與 attendee   ◀)) 349

attend：動詞，「出席」

attendee 或 attender：名詞，指出席者或在場者（不過，有些字，雖然字尾是 er 或 ee，但老外常常互為通用，就像：retirer = retiree; attender = attendee; escaper = escapee）

例句

· All meeting attendees（或 attenders）are encouraged to express their opinions.
鼓勵出席開會者發表意見。

» escaper 與 escapee   ◀)) 350

escape：動詞，逃脫

escaper 或 escapee：名詞，逃脫者

例句

· The escaper（或 escapee）was trying to escape the danger.
逃脫者設法逃脫危險。

retirer 與 retiree   🔊 351

retire：動詞，退休

retiree 或 retirer：名詞，指退休者

例句

· All retirees（或 retirers）should be well-treated.
所有退休者應該受到厚待。

Part 5　一些記單字的方法

　　據統計，英語中全部的單字約有 60 萬字左右，專家認為，只要了解常用的 2000 字，且能運用自如，就很不錯了。專業作家約要了解 5 萬字（約佔全部的 1/12），可見其餘的單字，可以「束之高閣」了。

　　然而，單字的記憶，或詞彙的擴充（to enlarge vocabulary）每個人的方式或與不同，以下介紹幾種常用的記憶方法，相信對於學習英文的過程能有所助益。

Part 5　一些記單字的方法

I. 由字首、字尾了解單字意義

1. 由字頭,也叫前綴（prefix）,能幫助了解單字的意義。一般而言,prefix 不能獨立使用,但以下也有一些所謂「假字頭」（pseudo prefix）,多由拉丁文演變而來,有時也可獨立使用。字頭後,有人加連字號（hyphen）也有人不加。

》 anti- 含有「防止」、「反對」、「反抗」（**against**）的意思　◀)) 352

例句

· Anti-abortion was a controversial issue during the political campaign.
　反墮胎在政治競選中,成為爭議的問題。

· Selfishness is the antipode of selflessness.
　自私恰恰是無私之反。
　（antipode 是恰恰相反的人或事）

· Mr. A is a weird and antisocial person.
　A 先生是位古怪且厭惡社交的人。（antisocial 反社會者）

其他

antimilitarism 反軍國主義；antiaircraft 防空；antipollution 防污染；anti-bacterial 抗菌劑；anticancer 抗癌；anti-rust 防鏽；anti-terrorism 反恐怖主義；antipoverty 反貧窮；anti-anxiety 抗焦慮；anti-freeze 防凍劑

有時 anti 也可獨立使用,意思是反對者。

>> **aqua-** 有「液體」、「水」（**water**）的意思。（有時也可獨立使用） 🔊 353

例句

· Mr. B bought a big aquarium for his living room.
B 先生為他的客廳買了一個大養魚缸。（aquarium 魚缸）

· Some colleges offer a course in aquaculture.
有些大學有水產養殖課程。（aquaculture 水產養殖）

其他

aqualung 水肺（水中呼吸器）；aquacade = aquashow 水上運動表演；aquaplane 滑水板（由快艇牽引，供人乘立的一種運動器具）；aquatel 水上旅館（由停在船塢的遊艇組成）

>> **auto-** 含有「本身」、「自動調整」或「自己」（**self**）的意思。（也可獨立使用，意思是汽車 = **automobile**） 🔊 354

例句

· Mrs. Wang prefers having a car with an automatic transmission.
王太太喜歡有自動變速器的汽車。（automatic 自動的）

· Some people demand regional autonomy.
有些人要求區域自治。（autonomy 自治）

其他

autography 親筆簽名；auto-alarm 自動報警器；auto-maker 汽車製造商；auto-worker 汽車工人；autocracy 獨裁統治

bi- 含有「兩次」或「雙面」（**two or double**）的意思。（不能獨立使用，是真正的 **prefix**） 355

例句

· Men and birds are bipeds.
　人和鳥是雙足動物。（biped 二足動物）

· This is a problem that poses bilateral difficulty.
　這是一個造成兩邊困難的問題。（bilateral 雙邊的）

> **其他**
>
> bifocals 雙光眼鏡；bicycle 自行車；bipod 雙腳架；biannual 一年兩次；bigamy 重婚；bicultural 二元文化；bicentennial 兩百週年紀念

bio- 含有「生物」、「生命」（**life**）的意思 356

例句

· Mr. B reads nothing but biographies of famous people.
　B 先生什麼不讀，只讀名人傳記。（biography 傳記）

· Many Chinese students earn Ph.D.s in biochemistry.
　許多中國學生取得生化博士學位。（biochemistry 生物化學）

> **其他**
>
> biogeography 生物地理學（研究生物的地理分佈）；bio-ecology 生物生態學；bio-mechanics 生物力學；bio-physics 生物物理學；bioclimatology 生物氣候學（研究氣候對生物的影響）
>
> 有時 bio 也可單獨使用 = biography，複數是 bios）

>> **co-**（或 **com-**）含有「聯合」、「有關」、「共同」（**together with**）的意思 🔊 357

例句

· John will cochair a meeting with Mary next week.
John 和 Mary 下週共同主持一次會議。（cochair 共同主持）

· It was not coincidental that the two women disappeared at the same time.
兩位婦女同時失蹤並非偶然。（coincidental 碰巧的）

其 他

coauthor 合著者；co-educational 男女同學的；coexistence 共存；coheir 共同繼承人；combination 結合；compile 彙編（compilation）；compress 壓緊（compression）等等。（有時 co. 獨立使用，是 company 或 county 的縮寫）

>> **circum-** 含有「周圍」或「環繞」（**surrounding**）的意思（**circum-** 不能獨立使用） 🔊 358

例句

· A joyful atmosphere circumfused the dancing party.
歡樂的氣氛籠罩著舞會。（circumfuse 充滿）

· Mr. Chang likes to talk in circumlocutions.
張先生喜歡拐彎抹角的說話。（circumlocution 迂迴說法）

其 他

circumstance 環境；circum-navigate 環繞航行；circumspect 周到的；circumvent 阻遏；circumlocution 婉轉；circumscribe 包圍、環繞

》 de- 含有「離開」、「取銷」、「分開」（**separate**）的意思。
（不能獨立使用） 🔊 359

例句

· The government will soon decentralize the nation's industry.
政府將分散該國的工業佈局。（decentralize 分散、權力下放）

· The scientist will demystify knowledge in order to help us to get know-how.
科學家將解開知識的神祕感，以幫助我們獲得技術常識。
（demystify 啟發，使人不再迷惑）

其 他

de-emphasize 不強調；decompress 減壓；defrost 除去冰霜；decontrol 解除控制；detract 減損（detraction）

》 dis- 含有「相反」、「缺乏」、「否定」（**not**）的意思 🔊 360

例句

· It will be difficult to persuade the superpowers to disarm.
要說服超級強權國家裁軍很難。（disarm 裁軍）

- If you send this nasty letter to your boss, you'll do yourself a disservice.
  如果你寄這封信給你的老闆，你會損害自己。（disservice 幫倒忙、損害）

- Many people show their dissatisfaction at the current economy.
  許多人不滿目前的經濟情況。（dissatisfaction 不滿意）

 其他

disapprove 不准；disorient 迷失方向；disgrace 失寵；disbelieve 不相信（disbelief）；disbar 取消律師資格；disfunction 機能障礙；disagree 不同意

» **ex-** 附在名詞前，表示「以前」、「前任」（**formerly**）的意思；但構成動詞時，則含有「超出」、「向外」（**beyond**）的意思

🔊 361

例句

- An excess of imports over exports worries some business people.
  貿易進口超過出口，令一些商人憂心。（excess 超越）

- Many people always exalt Nobel Prize laureates (to the skies).
  許多人把諾貝爾獎得主捧上了天。（exalt 高舉，升高）

 其他

ex-president 前任總統；ex-husband 前夫；export 出口；expand（expansion）擴大；exclude 不包括；expel 趕走；expatriate 流亡
（ex 可單獨使用，意思是已離婚的丈夫或妻子，或過去的情人）

>> **extra-** 通常附在形容詞前，表示「越出」或「超出」的意思。（獨立使用時，意思是額外的） 🔊 362

例句

· An ordinary person sometimes accomplishes some extraordinary things.
凡人有時能成就非凡的事情。（extraordinary 非凡的）

· Dr. A had an extra-marital affair with his nurse.
A 醫師與他的護士有婚外情。（extra-marital 婚外的）

其他

extracurricular 課外的；extrajudicial 法庭管轄之外的；
extrasensory 超感官的；extra-constitutional 憲法以外的；
extra-scientific 超科學的；extraterritorial 治外法權的

>> **hyper-** 含有「高於」、「超出」（**beyond or exceeding**）的意思
🔊 363

例句

· Mr. Wang's comment about his boss seemed to be hypercritical.
王先生對他老闆的批評，似乎很苛刻。（hypercritical 苛刻的）

· Some people are hypersensitive toward racial discrimination.
有些人對種族歧視非常敏感。（hypersensitive 非常過敏的）

其他

hypertension 高血壓；hypertensive 過度緊張；hyperspace 超
空間；hypersonic 高超音速的；hyperactive 極度活躍的
（有時 hyper 可獨立使用，當形容詞，意思是激動的）

》》 im-（或 **in-**）含有「無」、「不」（**not**）的意思　　◀》 364

例句

· Mr. A's criticism in this matter is rather impersonal.
A 先生對這件事的批評，並非針對某人。（impersonal 非個人的）

· Some old-fashioned people consider bikini immodest.
有些保守者認為比基尼式泳裝不端莊。（immodest 不端莊）

· His speech was inappropriate to this special situation.
他的演講不適合這個特殊情況。（inappropriate 不恰當）

其 他

imperfect 不完美的；immature 未成熟的；immortal 不朽的；
immeasurable 不可計量的；imbalance 不平衡的；inaccurate
不準確的；inescapable 逃避不了的；inhuman 無人性的
（im 不能獨立使用；in 單獨使用時，是介系詞，意思完全不同）

》》 inter- 含有「互相」、「在之間」（**between**）的意思　　◀》 365

例句

· There were several intercollegiate baseball games this year.
今年有幾次大學校際棒球賽。（intercollegiate 大學之間）

· We have many chances for interaction with female colleagues
in the office.
我們在辦公室與女同事有許多互動機會。（interaction 互動）

其他

interstate 州與州之間的；international 國際的；interpersonal 人際間的；interflow 交流；interplay 互相作用；interdependent 互相依賴的；interchange 交換

» **mis-** 含有「不當」、「不利」或「錯誤」（**wrongly**）的意思。 （不能獨立使用） 🔊) 366

例句

· Many high school students misbehave with teenage girls.
許多高中生與少女胡來。（**misbehave** 行為不端）

· Mr. C was indicted for misappropriating public funds.
C 先生因盜用公款而被提起公訴。（**misappropriate** 侵吞、挪用）

· Incompetent physicians will cause a high rate of misdiagnosis.
不勝任的醫生導致高誤診率。（**misdiagnosis** 誤診）

其他

misplace 放錯地方；misquote 錯誤引證；miscalculate 誤算；mistrust 不信任；mispronounce 發錯音；misdeed 罪行，惡行

» **mono-** 含有「單一」、「獨一」（**single**）的意思 🔊) 367

例句

· In many countries, tobacco is still a government monopoly.
在許多國家，菸草仍是政府專賣品。（**monopoly** 壟斷，專賣權）

· The English language has become international; few nations are monolingual.
英語變成國際性；很少國家只說單種語言。（monolingual 只使用一種語言）

monologue 獨白詞；monotone 單調；monorail 單軌鐵路；monodrama 單人劇；monogamy 一夫一妻制；monograph 專著、專論

>> **multi-** 含有「多的」、「多方面」（**many**）的意思。（不能單獨使用）

 368

例句

· Many U.S. colleges now offers multicultural courses.
許多美國大學現在有多文化的課程。（multicultural 多文化的）

· Mr. Wang has the ability to speak multidialectal Chinese.
王先生能說多種的中文方言。（multidialectal 多種方言）

multi-millionaire 千萬富翁；multibillion 數十億；multilingual 多語言的；multimedia 多媒體；multicolor 多彩

» **non-** 常用在名詞或形容詞前，表示「非」、「無」、「不是」（**not**）的意思。（不能獨立使用） 🔊 369

例句

· Libraries have many non-fiction and non-print materials.
圖書館有許多非小說類和非印刷品的資料。

· Many Chinese are known for being non-cooperative with their own fellow citizens.
許多老中不能與同胞合作，是出了名的。（non-cooperative 不合作）

其他

non-aggressive 無侵略性的；non-delivery 無法投遞；non-credit 無學分；nonexistence 不存在；nondairy 非乳製；non-commissioned 未受軍官銜的

» **over-** 含有「過份」、「超過」（**beyond**）的意思。（獨立使用時，當介詞、形容詞或副詞，意思不同） 🔊 370

例句

· Many young people today are exhausted from overwork.
現今許多年輕人因工作過度而疲憊不堪。（overwork 過度工作）

· There was a heavy overcast today.
今天是個多雲的陰天。（overcast 多雲，陰天）

其他

overload 超載；overflow 氾濫；overwhelm 壓倒，受不了；overheat 過度加熱；overdress 過份打扮；overdramatize 過份戲劇性的表達

>> **post-** 含有「後的」（**after**）的意義。（獨立使用時，意思是柱子、職位或郵政） 🔊 371

例句

· The ex-marine officer has received a posthumous award for his bravery.
這位曾任海軍陸戰隊軍官，因表現英勇而在死後獲獎。
（posthumous 死後的）

· Mr. Wang added a postscript to his letter.
王先生在他的信中附筆。（postscript 附筆）

postgraduate 研究生；postdoctorate 博士後研究人員；postwar 戰後；postnuptial 婚後的；postoperative 手術後

>> **pre-** 含有「在前」、「先於」（**before**）的意思。（不能獨立使用） 🔊 372

例句

· Teens should take all precautions against having car accidents.
年輕人應該採取一切防備，以免車禍。（precaution 預防）

· In Mr. Chen's mind, a wish to become wealthy has always predominated.
陳先生的心願，一直是發財致富。（predominate 主導，主宰）

precensor 預先審查； preoccupy 搶先佔有；predesignate 預先指定； premature 過早的成熟，比預期早；pre-requisite 前提，先決條件

>> **re-** 含有「重新」、「再次」、「回復」（**again**）的意思。（不能獨立使用）（**re.** 有時當作 **reference** 的縮寫） 🔊 373

例句

- The magician made the vanished bird reappear.
  魔術師把消失的鳥再度變出現。（**reappear** 再出現）

- Mr. Obama will readjust the U.S. foreign policy toward Cuba.
  歐巴馬先生將重新調整美國對古巴的外交政策。（**readjust** 重新調整）

其 他

rebound 彈回；reconfirm 再確定；redeem 贖回；reconfirm 再確定； recuperate 復原；reconstruct 重建； recall 回想起

>> **semi-** 含有「一部分」、「一半」（**half**）的意思 🔊 374

例句

- The teacher asked her students to stand in a semicircle.
  老師要她學生站成半圓形。（**semicircle** 半圓形）

- Her jewelry includes some semi-precious stones.
  她的首飾包括一些半寶石。（**semi-precious** 次貴重的）

其 他

semi-annual 半年一次；semi-monthly 半月一次、半月刊； semi-final 半決賽；semi-solid 半固體; semi-professional 半專業性；semi-automatic 半自動武器；semi-retirement 半退休狀態

» **super-** 含有「上方」、「超過」、「過份」（**over or above**）的
意思。（獨立使用時，多半當形容詞，意思是特級的，特大的）

🔊 375

例句

· I have been learning how to omit superfluous words in
writing.
我在學習如何刪去寫作的多餘字句。（**superfluous** 冗語，多餘的）

· Dr. A is the man with supercilious overconfidence.
A 醫生是目空一切、過於自信的人。（**supercilious** 高傲的）

其他

superhuman 超人的，超凡的；superabundance 極多，大量；
supersede 取代；superannuate 淘汰、解雇；supernatural 超
自然的

» **sub-** 含有「下面」、「從屬」、「底下」（**below**）的意思。
（**sub** 獨立使用時，意思是潛艇或地鐵）

🔊 376

例句

· The river overflowed and submerged the farm.
河水氾濫，淹沒了農田。（**submerge** 浸沒）

· The Information Bureau will prohibit some subversive
publications.
新聞局將禁止煽動性刊物。（**subversive** 暗中破壞）

其他

subcommittee 小組委員會；subconscious 下意識；submarine 潛水艇；substandard 在標準之下；sub-surface 地表下；subway 地鐵列車

» **tele-** 會有「電信」、「遠距離」（**far**）的意思。（不能獨立使用）　　🔊 377

例句

· The concert was televised nationally yesterday.
昨天音樂會是向全國轉播。（televise 用電視播放）

· The soldier was looking at the ship through his telescope.
士兵用望遠鏡察看船隻。

其他

telecommunication 電信；telemarketing 電話推銷；teleconference 電信會議； telephone 電話

» **trans-** 會有「超越」、「橫穿」（**across**）的意思　　🔊 378

例句

· You may leave the transaction of this matter to me.
你可以把這件事交我處理。（transaction 辦理）

· The doctor gave a blood transfusion to the patient.
醫生為病人輸血。（transfusion 灌輸）

其他

transmission 傳送；transoceanic 越洋的；transform 轉變；
transition 過渡時期；transplant 移植；transparency 透明；
transport 運輸

» un- 會有「相反」、「免去」、「沒有」（**not**）的意思　◀)) 379

例句

· Millions of Chinese war victims are uncompensated by the
Japanese government.
千百萬的中國戰爭受害者，沒有得到日本政府的賠償。
（**uncompensated** 未得補償的）

· Many high-ranking officials are unapproachable to ordinary
citizens.
許多高官很難親近平民。（**unapproachable** 難以親近的）

 其他

unconditional 無條件的；unbalance 不平衡；unattractive
無吸引力的；uncommon 不平常；undecided 未決定的；
unacceptable 不能接受的；unavailable 達不到的；uncover 揭露

2. 由字尾、也叫後綴（**suffix**），也能幫助了解字的意思。（以下單字使用 a. v. n. adv. 分別代表形容詞、動詞、名詞和副詞）

最常見的字尾有：

» **-able** 附在動詞或名詞後構成形容詞，會有「適於」、「易於」、「能夠」（**capable of**）的意思。有些單字需要重複或改變最後一個字母，再接上後綴。　🔊 **380**

例句

· Certain portions of his income are not taxable.
他的某些收入不應課稅。（**taxable** 應納稅的）

· This river is swimmable.
這個河是適合游泳的。

其他

payable 應支付的； enjoyable 有興趣的；readable 可讀性很強的； eatable 可吃的；fashionable 流行的； breakable 易破的；inflammable 易燃的； considerable 值得考慮的，重大的

» **-ance**（或 **ence**）附在動詞後構成名詞。含有「行動」、「過程」、「狀況」（**circumstance**）的意思　🔊 **381**

例句

· The singer made her first appearance in concert.
演唱會中這位女歌手首次登台。

- Much to my annoyance, he failed to keep his word.
  他不守信，令我惱怒。

- His major problem is his dependence on drugs.
  他的最大問題是依賴吸毒。

- There is a lack of correspondence between his promises and his actions.
  他的諾言和行動缺乏一致。

performance 進行； attendance 出席；conveyance 運送； acceptance 接受；existence 存在； difference 差異；conference 商談；inference 推斷
（以上單字，如把 -ance 和 -ence 去掉，都成為動詞）

» -ant（或 -ent）構成名詞或形容詞時，含有「動作」、「處於」、「施行者」、「性質」（**have the quality of**）的意思　◀) 382

例句

- Mr. B should be repentant for what he has done to his family.
  B 先生應該替他對家庭的所做所為，感到後悔。

- The boy looked so triumphant that I knew he had won the game.
  男孩得意洋洋，我知道他比賽贏了。

- Many writers take different approaches to (in) learning.
  許多作家採取不同的學習方法。

- Gasoline is a solvent (liquid) to remove grease spots.
  去除油污，汽油有溶解力。

其他

expectant 滿心期待的； trenchant 尖銳的；absorbent 能吸收的；confident 有信心的；assistant 助手 (*n.*)； coolant 冷卻劑 (*n.*)；servant 服務生 (*n.*)

» -ate 構成動詞時，含有「產生」、「成為」的意思；構成名詞時，有「職務」的意思；構成形容詞，有「充滿的」、「有關的」的意思

🔊 383

例句

· Mr. A gave a passionate speech last night.
　昨晚 A 先生發表一場熱情的演說。（passionate (*a.*)）

· John was the American consulate in Shanghai.
　John 是在上海的美國領事。（consulate (*n.*)）

· Too much worry may ulcerate his stomach.
　太多的擔憂，也許會使他胃潰瘍。（ulcerate 產生潰瘍 (*v.*)）

其他

collegiate 大學的； expatriate 移居、流亡 (*n.*)；motivate 激起 (*v.*)； validate 使生效 (*v.*)；activate 使活動起來 (*v.*)

» -ful 附在動詞或名詞後，構成形容詞，含有「顯出」、「特性」、「充滿」（full）的意思

🔊 384

例句

· The older people tend to become forgetful.
　老人有變健忘的趨勢。

· It was very thoughtful of you to make this arrangement for me.
你為我做這安排，是很體貼的。

其他

scornful 輕蔑的，嘲笑的；masterful 專橫的，好支配人的；eventful 多事的；joyful 快樂的；bountiful 充足的；hateful 可恨的
但是，handful 一把、麻煩事；cupful 一滿杯；roomful 一屋子的人，都是名詞，不是形容詞，也可有複數，如 handsful 或 handfuls）

例句

· His hair begins to fall out in handfuls.
他的頭髮一把一把的脫落。

» -fy 構成動詞，會有「使成為」、「使具有」（**make or become**）
的意思   🔊 385

例句

· Mr. A's explanation may clarify the situation.
A 先生的解釋，能澄清狀況。

· His job performance does not satisfy his boss.
他的工作表現，不能滿足他的老闆。

其他

liquefy 或 liquify 使液化；glorify 使光榮、頌揚；beautify 使美化起來；putrefy 使靡爛、化膿、使墮落；crucify 把手腳釘在十字架上、迫害

» **-ible** 構成形容詞，會有「能被」、「可成」（**having condition of**）的意思　　　　　　　　　　🔊 386

例句

· Old people need to eat more digestible food.
老年人要吃比較容易消化的食物。

· Generally, hearsay is not permissible evidence in court.
通常，道聽塗說在法庭上不許作為證據。

其他

flexible 有彈性的；accessible 易接近的；edible 可食用的；reversible 可翻轉的；convertible 可轉化的；eligible 合格的；incredible 難以置信的；sensible 明智，合情理的

» **-ish** 含有「稍有」、「似乎」、「趨向」、「一些」的意思　🔊 387

例句

· Mr. A's behavior seems (to be) a little childish.
A 先生的行為似乎有點幼稚。

· He is a fortyish man with a pleasing personality.
他是位四十歲左右的男子，擁有令人快樂的個性。

其他

girlish 女孩似的；bookish 好讀書的、書呆子氣；sweetish 略甜的；foolish 愚蠢的；thirtyish 卅歲左右、三〇年代的；selfish 自私的；reddish 帶有紅色的，淡紅的

» **-ism** 構成抽象名詞時，含有「主義」、「特性」、「病態」、「信仰」等意思。 🔊 388

例句

· The boy received Christian baptism last week.
  這個男孩上週接受基督教的洗禮。

· Bob's heroism in saving the drowning girl from the river was highly praised.
  Bob 從河中救出落水女孩的英勇行為受到高度讚揚。

其他

Americanism 崇美主義；barbarism 野蠻或落後狀態；skepticism = scepticism 懷疑態度；Nationalism 民族主義；alcoholism 酗酒；Mongolism 蒙古症、唐氏症；progressivism 進步黨主義

» **-ist** 構成名詞時，有「實行者」、「信仰者」、「專家」 🔊 389
  （**specialist**）的意思

例句

· Mary wants to be a pianist in her career.
  Mary 要以鋼琴家為她事業。

· Being a perfectionist, Mr. B makes his life more stressful.
  B 先生是位完美主義者，使得生活壓力更大。
  （perfectionist 事事求全、完美主義者）

其 他

tourist 旅遊者； journalist 新聞工作者；botanist 植物學家；
organist 風琴手；moralist 道德家； oncologist 腫瘤（癌症）
醫生；violinist 小提琴手； socialist 社會主義者

》 **-ity** 多半為名詞，含有「狀態」、「特性」、「程度」的意思

🔊 390

例句

・A police officer has the authority to arrest law-breakers.
警察有權逮捕犯法者。（authority 權力）

・The long-standing animosities between Taiwan and China
should be ended.
台灣與大陸長期存在的敵意應該終止。（animosity 仇恨，敵意）

其 他

intensity 強烈，極度；possibility 可能性；community 社區；
seniority 年長，資深；temerity 魯莽，冒失

》 **-ive** 構成形容詞時，含有「屬於」、「有關」的意思　　🔊 391

例句

・He asked a question in an interrogative tone.
他以疑問的口氣提出問題。（interrogative 疑問的）

・No substantive progress was made during the first negotiation.
第一輪的協商，沒有取得實際進展。（substantive 實際的，重大的）

其 他

active 活躍的；amusive 有趣的；selective 選擇性的；
defective 有缺點的；supportive 支持的

» **-ize** 由名詞或形容詞構成動詞時，含有「使形成」、「產生」、
「成為」的意思　　　　　　　　　　　　　　　　🔊 392

例句

· The preacher baptized Mary in Church last Sunday.
上星期天牧師為 Mary 洗禮。（baptize (*v.*) 給施禮；baptism 洗禮
式 (*n.*)）

· Mr. A apologized profusely to her for being rude.
A 先生因粗野而一再向她致歉。（apologize (*v.*) 道歉； apology
(*n.*)）

其 他

· memorize (*v.*) 記住（memory (*n.*) 記憶）
· materialize (*v.*) 使具體化（material (*n.*) 材料）
· systemize (*v.*) 使系統化（system (*n.*) 系統）
· monopolize (*v.*) 壟斷、獨佔（monopoly (*n.*) 專賣）
· equalize (*v.*) 使平等（equal (*a.*) 平等的）
· popularize (*v.*) 使大眾化（popular (*a.*) 流行的）
· economize (*v.*) 節省（economic (*a.*) 經濟學的）
· centralize (*v.*) 作為中心（central (*a.*) 中心的）

» **-less** 多半附在名詞後，構成形容詞，含有「不」或「無」（**not**）的意思 🔊 393

例句

· It was careless of her to leave her bag in the bus.
她把袋子留在公車上，很不小心。

· Mr. B is very kind but rather humorless.
B 先生很親切但缺乏幽默。

> ageless 不顯老的；limitless 無限制的；carless 無車的；
> doubtless 無疑的；valueless 無價值的；tireless 不疲倦的；
> homeless 無家可歸的

» **-ly** 構成副詞時，含有「方式」、「程度」、「範圍」的意思

🔊 394

例句

· I tried mightily to lift the heavy box.
我竭盡全力地想舉起重的箱子。（mighty (*a.*) 強大的）

· The neighborhood became oddly silent last night.
昨晚鄰居奇特地安靜。（odd (*a.*) 奇特的）

> smilingly 微笑地；swiftly 快速地；unexpectedly 意外地；
> outwardly 外表地；slowly 慢慢地；relatively 相對地
>
> 但 -ly 若附在名詞後，構成形容詞時，則含有某種「特性」的意思。

例句

· Mrs. A shows motherly kindness to her friends.
A 太太對她的朋友顯出慈母般的愛心。

· Many people are paid on an hourly basis.
許多人是按鐘點計酬。

其他

brotherly (*a.*) 兄弟般的；kingly (*a.*) 國王似的，高貴的；
heavenly (*a.*)天國的，超凡的；ghostly (*a.*) 似鬼的

» -ment 多半附在動詞，構成名詞，有「行動」、「結果」、「手
段」的意思   ◀⃝ 395

例句

· A person who needs to be employed is seeking employment.
需要被雇用的人，就是找工作。（ employ (*v.*) ）

· When you judge his actions, you are making a judgement.
（ = judgment ）
當你評價他的行為時，你就是在作出判斷。（ judge (*v.*) ）

其他

amazement 驚奇；confinement 限制、禁閉；refreshment
恢復活力的事物、茶點、便餐；encirclement 環繞、包圍；
postponement 延期
（以上單字，如把 -ment 去掉，都成為動詞）

» **-ness** 附在形容詞後，構成抽象名詞時，會有「狀態」、「性質」、
「程度」的意思 ◀) 396

 例句

· He said that everything was in a state of preparedness.
他說一切準備就緒。（prepared (*a.*) 準備好的狀態）

· Only laziness will prevent me from writing articles.
唯有懶惰才使我不寫文章。（lazy (*a.*)）

其他

sadness 悲傷（sad (*a.*)）；goodness 美德、善良（good
(*a.*)）；kind-heartedness 仁慈、好心（kind-hearted (*a.*)）；
fierceness 殘酷、兇猛（fierce (*a.*)）

» **-or**（或 **-er**）構成名詞時，會有「人」或「物」（**person or thing**）
的意思 ◀) 397

 例句

· Some hospitals have been looking for liver donors.
有些醫院在尋求肝臟捐贈人。（donor 捐贈者）

· The two-star general was invited to be a spectator at the
military parade.
二星將官受邀參觀閱兵遊行。（spectator 旁觀者）

其他

actor 演員；counsellor 或 counselor 諮詢、顧問、指導老師；
conductor嚮導、樂隊指揮；error 差錯；generator 發電機；
tractor 拖拉機；runner 賽跑者；player 球員

» -ous 構成形容詞時，含有「如同」、「具有」的意思　🔊 398

例句

· We are all dubious about the whole thing.
我們對整個事情，都很懷疑。（dubiety (n.) 懷疑）

· It was courageous for him to oppose his boss.
他大膽地反對他的老闆。（courage (n.) 勇氣）

envious 妒忌的、羨慕的（envy (*n.*)）；mountainous 多山
的（mountain (*n.*)）；poisonous 有毒的 （poison (*n.*)）；
thunderous 打雷般的（thunder (*n.*)）； bigamous 重婚的
（bigamy (*n.*)）

» -tion（或 -sion）構成名詞時，有「結果」、「動作」、「狀態」
的意思　　　　　　　　　　　　　　　　🔊 399

例句

· A high crime rate can be a reflection of an unstable society.
高犯罪率是一種社會不安的反映。（reflect (*v.*)）

· China's Great Wall is one of great tourist attractions of the
world.
中國的萬里長城是偉大的世界旅遊勝地之一。（attract (*v.*)）

其他

absorption 吸收（absorb (*v.*)）；affliction 苦惱、折磨（afflict (*v.*)）；adaptation 適應、改編（adapt (*v.*)）；exploration 探險、勘探（explore (*v.*)）；prediction 預料（predict (*v.*)）；discussion 討論（discuss (*v.*)）；confusion 混亂（confuse (*v.*)）

II. 同義字、反義字、同音異義字

利用歸屬語典（thesaurus），可以幫助了解同義字、反義字、和同音異義字。

① 同義字（synonyms）括弧內是意義相近的字。　　🔊 400

例句

· Mr. A's retirement benefits are **adequate** (→ **enough**) to make a living.
A 先生的退休福利夠他生活。

· I admire those people who show **loyalty** (→ **faithfullness**) to their families.
我很欽佩那些對家庭很忠誠的人。

其他

· efficient 效率高的、有能力的（capable）
· banish 放逐（exile）
· benevolence 善意（kindness）

- hesitant 猶豫的（reluctant）
- disclose 透露（reveal）
- harmony 和諧（balance）
- nice 好的（amiable）
- negligent 疏忽的（careless）
- censor 審查（restrict）
- donation 奉獻（contribution）
- relinquish 放棄（abandon）
- hypocrite 偽君子（pretender）
- vague 含糊的，不明確的（ambiguous）

2. 反義字（antonyms）就是意義相反的單字。括弧內是反義字。

🔊 401

例句

- Many big shots are arrogant but some are surprisingly humble.
  許多大人物很驕傲，有些則出乎意外的謙虛。
  arrogant 高傲的（⟷ **humble**）

- Mr. A is generous in helping others but Mr. B is very stingy.
  A 先生慷慨助人，但 B 先生小氣巴拉。
  generous 慷慨的（⟷ **stingy**）

其他

- frugal 節省的（⟷ wasteful）
- oppose 反抗（⟷ defend）
- negative 消極的（⟷ positive）

- shallow 淺的（↔ deep）
- sharp 鋒利的（↔ dull）
- praise 讚揚（↔ blame）
- random 任意的（↔ deliberate）
- vertical 垂直的（↔ horizontal 橫的、水平的）
- order 順序（↔ confusion 混淆）
- feeble 軟弱的（↔ sturdy）
- careful 小心的（↔ negligent）
- veracity 真實性（↔ falsehood）

③. 同音異義字（**homonyms**）兩個字的發音相同或相似，但意義和拼法不同。　🔊 402

例句

- The words stationary and stationery have the same pronunciation, but different meanings.
  （stationary 固定的；stationery 文具、信紙）
- Although capitol and capital are pronounced the same, they differ in meaning.
  （capitol 美國國會大廈；capital 首都、資金、大寫字母）

其　他

- altar (*n.*) 聖壇；alter (*v.*) 改變
- holy (*a.*) 神聖的；wholly (*adv.*) 完全地
- knight (*n.*) 武士；night (*n.*) 夜晚
- waste (*v.*) 浪費；waist (*n.*) 腰部

- tale (*n.*) 故事、傳說；tail (*n.*) 尾巴
- steal (*v.*) 偷盜；steel (*n.*) 鋼鐵
- pair (*n.*) 一雙；pare (*v.*) 修剪、削去
- rap (*v.*) 奪取、敲出聲；wrap (*v.*) 包紮
- raze (*v.*) 折毀；raise (*v.*) 舉起
- main (*a.*) 主要的；mane (*n.*) 馬鬃、密髮
- sun (*n.*) 太陽；son (*n.*) 兒子
- whether 或者、是否；weather (*n.*) 天氣
- whole (*adj. / n.*) 全部；hole (*n.*) 破洞

III. 組合字（**combined words**） 403

有些字是由兩個單字組成。

例句

- Mr. A planned to hitchhike through Europe.
  A 先生計畫在路上搭便車遊遍歐洲。（**hitch + hike → hitchhike**）

- The manufacturers are making more foldaway and feather weight bikes for people to carry around.
  廠商製造更多可摺疊又輕便的單車，以便人們到處攜帶。
  （**fold + away → foldaway** (*a.*) 可摺疊的）
  （**feather** 羽毛 **+ weight** 重量 **→ featherweight** (*a.*) 極輕的）

其 他

- wastewater 廢水（waste 廢物 + water）
- copycat 模仿者（copy 模仿 + cat）
- searchlight 探照燈（search 搜尋 + light）
- backpack 背包（back + pack）
- thumbtack 圖釘（thumb + tack）
- newscast 新聞廣播（news + cast）
- landfill 垃圾掩埋場（land + fill）
- network 網絡（net + work）
- sandpaper 砂紙（sand + paper）
- matchmaker 火柴製造商、媒人（match (*n.*) 火柴、配對 + maker 製造者）
- takeover 接受（take + over）
- joystick 飛機駕駛桿（joy + stick）

IV. 創製字（invented words）

◀)) 404

有些單字原由組合而創製而成的新字。

例句

- Some rich women splurge on diamond rings and mink coats.
  有些富婆在鑽戒和貂皮外套上揮霍金錢。
  （splurge 花大錢：splash (*v.*) 潑灑 + surge (*n./v.*) 猛衝、浪湧）

- The man was twiddling his thumbs waiting for the bus to arrive.
  男子閒著無聊旋弄兩手大拇指等公車來。
  （twiddle (*v.*) 擺弄（twitch 抽動 + fiddle 不經意地作事）

其 他

- brunch 早午餐 （breakfast 早餐 + lunch 午餐）
- moped 機器腳踏車 （motor 機動 + pedal 踏板、騎腳踏車）
- smog 煙霧 （smoke 煙 + fog 霧）
- radar 雷達 （radio detecting 無線偵測 + ranging 涉及範圍）
- twirl 轉動 （twist 扭轉 + whirl 迴旋）
- gasohol 混有百分之十酒精的汽油 （gasoline + alcohol）
- hi-fi 高音響設備 （high fidelity 高保真度）
- flu 流行性感冒 （influenza 的簡短說法）
- bike 腳踏車 （bicycle 的簡短說法）
- technophobe 技術恐懼 （technology + phobia）

V. 字尾的一些規則　　　　　　　　　　　　　🔊 405

1. 遇到字尾是 y，而 y 前面是子音，則把 y 改為 i，再加上後綴
（suffix）

例句

vary (*v.*) 改變	various (*a.*) 不同的
snappy (*a.*) 厲聲說話	snappily (*adv.*) 厲聲地
rely (*v.*) 依靠	reliance (*n.*) 信賴
merry (*a.*) 歡樂的	merriment (*n.*) 歡樂
defy (*v.*) 公然反抗	defiant (*a.*) 反抗的
lazy (*a.*) 懶散的	lazily (*adv.*) 懶散地

mystery (*n.*) 神秘事物	mysterious (*a.*) 神秘的
study (*v.*)(*n.*) 學習	studious (*a.*) 勤學的
melody (*n.*) 美妙音樂	melodious (*a.*) 旋律優美的
greedy (*a.*) 貪心的	greedily (*adv.*) 貪心地

但字尾是 y，而 y 前面是母音，則可直接加後綴：

例句

pay (*v.*) 付錢	payable (*a.*) 應支付的
joy (*n.*) 喜悅	joyous (*a.*) 高興的
play (*v.*) 玩耍	playful (*a.*) 愛玩耍的、開玩笑的
toy (*n.*) 玩具	toyish (*a.*) 玩具似的、不重要的

但有例外：

day (*n.*) 白天	daily (*a.*) 每天的
gay (*a.*) 愉快的	gaily (*adv.*) 愉快的

2. 有些字尾是 e 的字，要刪去 e，再加有母音的後綴

例句

adore (*v.*) 愛慕	adorable (*a.*) 可敬愛的、可愛的
care (*n.*) 掛心	caring (*a.*) 關心的
create (*v.*) 創造	creative (*a.*) 有創造力的
move (*v.*) 移動	movable (*a.*) 可移動的
use (*v.*) 使用	usable (*a.*) 可用的
love (*v.*) 愛	lovable (*a.*) 可愛的

desire (*n.*) 慾望	desirable (*a.*) 令人喜歡的、富有魅力的
ignore (*v.*) 忽視	ignorance (*n.*) 無知
value (*n.*) 價值	valuable (*a.*) 貴重的
imagine (*v.*) 想像	imaginary (*a.*) 想像中的
guide (*v.*) 指導	guidance (*n.*) 指導
argue (*v.*) 爭論	argument (*n.*) 爭論
arrive (*v.*) 到達	arrival (*n.*) 到達
expense (*n.*) 花費	expensive (*a.*) 昂貴的

但也有字尾是 e，但可直接加後綴的字：

change (*v.*) 更改	changeable (*a.*) 易變的
peace (*n.*) 安寧	peaceable (*a.*) 和平的、平和的
hate (*n.*) 恨	hateful (*a.*) 可恨的
arrange (*v.*) 安排	arrangement (*n.*) 整理
hope (*n.*) 希望	hopeful (*a.*) 充滿希望的
close (*v.*) 關閉	closeness (*v.*) 密切關係
late (*a.*) 遲的	lately (*adv.*) 最近、近來

當然，也有例外：

| true (*a.*) 真實的 | truly (*adv.*) 真誠的 |

（加的後綴 -ly 沒有母音，但是還是去字尾 e）

2. 有的字尾是子音，而子音前面是短母音，那麼要重複字尾的子音後，再加後綴（suffix）

例句

（許多是動詞的時態變化）

---

bat (*v.*) 用球棒猛擊 （batted, batting）

pat (*v.*) 輕拍 （patted, patting）

tap (*v.*) 輕敲 （tapped, tapping）

slip (*v.*) 滑動、滑跤 （slipped, slipping）

slam (*v.*) 使勁關上 （slammed, slamming）

omit (*v.*) 省略 （omitted, omitting）

permit (*v.*) 允許 （permitted, permitting）

trim (*v.*) 修剪 （trimmed, trimming）

ship (*v.*) 船運 （shipped, shipping）

drop (*v.*) 掉下 （dropped, dropping）

knit (*v.*) 編結 （knitted, knitting）

swim (*v.*) 游泳 （swimming; swimmer 游泳者）

run (*v.*) 跑步 （running; runner 跑步者）

win (*v.*) 獲勝 （winning; winner 優勝者）

forget (*v.*) 忘記 （forgetting; forgetter 健忘者）

IV. 容易混淆的字尾　　　　　　　🔊 406

1. 字尾是 -cede、-ceed、-sede

例句

（多半是動詞）

accede 答應	concede 承認
precede 先於	secede 分離
intercede 說情	recede 後退
exceed 超過	proceed 繼續進行
succeed 成功	supersede 取代

2. 字尾是 -ance、-ence

例句

（多半是名詞）

abundance 豐富	acquaintance 認識的人、相識
appearance 出現	brilliance 光輝
defiance 違抗	importance 重要
radiance 發光	resonance 回聲
romance 浪漫、愛情	tolerance 忍受
absence 缺席	convenience 方便
correspondence 符合、通信	difference 差別
excellence 卓越	independence 獨立
patience 忍耐、耐心	presence 在場
reference 參考	violence 暴力

VII. 容易拼錯的常用單字

aerial 航空的	aisle 通道、走道
amateur 業餘愛好者	anecdote 趣聞、軼事

avenue 大道	awkward 笨拙的、尷尬的
antenna 天線	bulletin 公告欄
bureau 辦事處	banquet 宴會
calendar 日曆	conceit 自負
chauffeur 私人司機	counterfeit 偽冒品
colonel 上校	condemn 譴責
conscientious 認真的	deceive 欺騙
defendant 被告	dessert 甜點
embarrass 尷尬、使窘迫	emergency 緊急情況
environment 環境	envelope 信封
exaggerate 誇大	foreign 外國的
fierce 兇猛的	government 政府
guarantee 保證	hygiene 衛生
knowledge 知識	leisure 悠閒
lieutenant 陸軍中尉	lightning 閃電
millionaire 百萬富翁	mediocre 中等、平庸
ninety 九十	parallel 平行線
perceive 察覺	physician 醫生
permanent 永久	perspiration 汗水
privilege 特權	receipt 收到
prairie 草原	pronunciation 發音
rhythm 節律、韻律	rhetoric 修辭學、辭令
spaghetti 義大利細麵	souvenir 紀念品
temperament 氣質、性格	temperature 溫度
temporary 暫時的	thorough 徹底的
vacuum 真空	villain 惡棍、流氓
weird 鬼怪的	width 寬度
yield 產量、讓路	

VIII. 善用字典

使用一本好字典，可幫助瞭解詞類的變化，也能知道同樣一個字，有幾個不同的意思和用法。

例句

舉 **bear** 作例子

- The patient can hardly bear the pain.
  病人幾乎不能忍受疼痛。
  （**bear** = tolerate (*v.*) 忍受）

- Please bear the injured man to the ambulance.
  請把傷患抬到救護車上。
  （**bear** = carry (*v.*) 運送）

- This shelf didn't bear the weight of these boxes.
  這架子不能承受這些箱子的重量。
  （**bear** = support (*v.*) 支撐）

- That big bear in the zoo can be dangerous.
  動物園裡的那隻大熊可能具危險性。
  （**bear** 在這是名詞，大熊）

再舉 **fast** 作例子：

- Her bike got stuck fast between the bushes.
  她的單車緊緊地卡在叢樹中。
  （**fast** = firmly (*adv.*) 穩固地，**fast** 也可當形容詞）

- The clock is always five minutes fast.
  這個鐘總是快五分鐘。
  （**fast** = quick (*adv.*) 快速地，**fast** 也可當形容詞，形容快速）

・Many people prefer eating tender steak.
　許多人愛吃嫩牛排。
　（tender (*a.*) 嫩的）

・Mr. A will tender his resignation next week.
　A 先生下週將提出辭呈。
　（tender (*v.*) 正式提出）

・Only a few people were present at the meeting yesterday.
　昨天只有幾個人到場開會。
　（present (*a.*) 有出席的）

・He will present a pricy present to his girlfriend.
　他要送給女朋友昂貴的禮物。
　（第一個 present 是動詞，贈送；第二個 present 是名詞，禮物）
　pricy (*a.*) 昂貴，也拼成 pricey）

　此外，建議每天隨身攜帶一些單字卡，正面寫單字，反面寫該字的
　意思和用法，時時練習，這是許多人記單字的方法。

Linking English

如何活用日常英文單字？

2012年8月初版　　　　　　　　　　　　　定價：新臺幣320元
有著作權・翻印必究
Printed in Taiwan.

著　　　者	懷　　　　　中
發 行 人	林　　載　　爵

出　版　者	聯經出版事業股份有限公司	叢書編輯	李　　　　　芃
地　　　　址	台北市基隆路一段180號4樓	內文排版	安　　琪　　琳
編輯部地址	台北市基隆路一段180號4樓	封面設計	Lilly Lai
叢書主編電話	(02)87876242轉226	錄音後製	純粹錄音後製公司
台北聯經書房	台北市新生南路三段94號		
電　　　　話	(02)23620308		
台中分公司	台中市北區健行路321號1樓		
暨門市電話	(04)22371234ext.5		
郵政劃撥帳戶第	0100559-3號		
郵撥電話	(02)23620308		
印　刷　者	文聯彩色製版印刷有限公司		
總　經　銷	聯合發行股份有限公司		
發　行　所	台北縣新店市寶橋路235巷6弄6號2樓		
電　　　　話	(02)29178022		

行政院新聞局出版事業登記證局版臺業字第0130號

本書如有缺頁，破損，倒裝請寄回台北聯經書房更換。　　ISBN　978-957-08-4029-2 (平裝)
聯經網址：www.linkingbooks.com.tw
電子信箱：linking@udngroup.com

國家圖書館出版品預行編目資料

如何活用日常英文單字？/懷中著.
初版．臺北巿．聯經．2012年8月（民101年）.
320面．14.8×21公分（Linking English）
ISBN　978-957-08-4029-2（平裝附光碟）

1.英語　2.詞彙

805.12　　　　　　　　　　　　　101012797